BEAUTY'S CURSED SLEEP

A SLEEPING BEAUTY FAIRYTALE RETELLING

THE CURSED BEAUTY SERIES
BOOK ONE

MARY E. TWOMEY

MARY E. TWOMEY, LLC

BEAUTY'S CURSED SLEEP

Book One in the Cursed Beauty Series

By

Mary E. Twomey

COPYRIGHT

Copyright © 2018 Mary E. Twomey, LLC
Cover Art by Shayne Leighton
of Parliament House Book Designs

All rights reserved.
First Edition: May 2018

This is a work of fiction. Any resemblance of characters to actual persons, living or dead, is purely coincidental. The author holds exclusive rights to this work. Unauthorized duplication is prohibited.

This book is licensed for your personal enjoyment only. If you would like to share this book with another person, please purchase an additional copy for each reader. Thank you for respecting the hard work of this author.

For information:
http://www.maryetwomey.com

DEDICATION

For Sunday

May your dreams never be small.

RORY JOHNSTONE'S SHORTENED LIFE

"I don't have a Pulse," Rory admitted, smoothing her long, dark hair over her shoulder with a brush of her left hand. She clicked her pen three times in her right fist, as if that would make the conversation less awkward. Did she wish she could Pulse emotions or abilities into others, as everyone else in the magical community could do? Sure. But she couldn't, so the fact that every month she had to check in with the council and report back the big news of absolutely nothing felt like a regularly scheduled stab to the chest. "Are you quite finished? I have to get back to work."

She glanced across the desk at her uncle, keeping their mirrored sigh inaudible so the speakerphone didn't pick up on notes of exasperation. Frustration only fueled certain members of the council, and she didn't want to give them any further fodder.

The superior lilt of the man on the phone made Rory cringe. "Patience, Aurora. I'm making a note. Another month, and still no Pulse. My, my. Most of us find our Pulse by age seven. How old are you now?"

Rory's uncle's upper lip curved slightly at the not-so-subtle needling that happened during these calls. He leaned back in the black leather swivel chair of his no-frills office. Though Remus was thirty-six, he glared at the phone, as if that would make the slow humiliation for his niece end sooner.

Rory bit back the urge to tell off the Baron. He knew very well how old she was. He'd known her since she was a baby. She'd endured his insipid political jokes over and over at the Dinners of the Elite, all with a polite smile on her face. "I'm twenty-four."

"Four months left before Malaura's curse is rumored to come into your life. Wouldn't it be lovely to find your Pulse *before* it's predicted to slow?"

Rory's uncle usually wore a breezy smile to counter his commanding office demeanor, but Rory could see the vein popping out along his temple, marking his notable stress. As much as she despised these phone calls, her failures were every bit as much a reflection on him for not producing a brightly shining star student to present to all of Avondale.

Rory stiffened at the low blow. "I don't believe in curses, least of all my own. You're in your sixties, Baron," she scolded him. "That's old enough to put such childish superstitions behind you. Are you still putting your dentures under your pillow in hopes the tooth fairy will leave you with some spare change?"

The Baron could dole out the insults without threat of conscience, but when it came to dealing with the family who had never cowered to him, he was left bereft of acerbic comebacks. "Young lady, it's no wonder you're... I can't believe the daughter of the Chancellor would speak to me like... You'd better pray your curse doesn't come to fruition. Being woken by true love's kiss only works if someone can tolerate your mouth."

Rory's tone was light and airy, as if she hadn't just stepped up to the plate to play hardball with the conniving man most of the council cowered to. "Speaking of true loves, how is your son these days? I haven't seen Calvin in a while. Tell him I'll return his many calls soon. You know how busy life can get."

It was a subtle needling, but to be fair, the Baron had started it.

Rory's uncle took hold of the conversation before it spiraled out of control. "Is that all, Baron?"

"For now. Remus, you are without a doubt, the most disappointing tutor I've ever met. Your pupil has made absolutely no progress, and..."

Remus put the receiver back in its cradle, sniggering at Rory's gasp at the outright defiance. "Oh, he's going to be mad you hung up on him."

"No more angry than he'll be that Calvin is still calling

you all the time. Can you imagine the scandal? The Baron's son hooking up with a girl who doesn't have a Pulse." He shook his head and tsked her. "What would the neighbors say?" His upper lip pulled in disgust once more. Remus slid a stack of papers into a folder, turning his focus back to the work at-hand.

Guilt and shame washed through Rory, as they always did after these monthly phone calls. "You're a wonderful tutor, Remus. The Baron was out of line, criticizing you like that."

Remus nodded, offering up a seemingly unaffected smile at his niece. He rolled his broad shoulders and brushed his hand down his green tie, which turned blue after one swipe – a thing he often did when he was thinking things he wouldn't say aloud. "I know. And you're an excellent student. Some things just weren't meant to be, and we're not going to waste our time beating ourselves up about it all. Understood?"

Rory's head bobbed, but she clicked her pen three times, as she often did when she felt unsettled in irreparable ways. She didn't speak, but rather internalized everything, tucking the Baron's icy words in her heart for use in future self-flagellation.

"Hey, chin up. Where are you? You're going to a bad place in your mind."

She bit down on her plump lower lip. "Honestly? I'm worried about the annual exam at the end of the month. I'm supposed to be able to levitate a teacup by then, but it's been too many years of failing the test. Why do they put me through the humiliation every year? They wouldn't care as much if I wasn't the Chancellor's daughter. They'd let me be a Deadpulse, and be done with it." Then she hung her head, her lean shoulders drooping. "I can't even levitate a teacup. Totally embarrassing. There are grade school children who can make teacups *and* their saucers lift off the table, the teacups filled to the brim without spilling a drop."

"A totally useful skill for work at a Foundation," Remus simpered not unkindly. "Your Pulse will come when it comes." He was only twelve years older than her, and the two shared more of a big-brother-little-sister rela-tionship than anything else – comforting and challenging each other as needed.

"And if it doesn't?" Her eyes flicked to his, revealing a portion of the raw underbelly she tried never to expose in mixed company. "If my biggest dream never comes true?"

Remus raised his chin, in hopes that someday his niece wouldn't have to work so hard to keep her own chin lifted. "This is your biggest dream?" He pointed to the pen on his desk, and with barely any effort at all, it raised up, as if giving itself to him as an offering of subservience. Then the pen collapsed back onto the desk, bereft of the magic that had bewitched it into motion. Remus' eyebrows pushed together in frustration. "Your dreams are small. I can't imagine anything more tragic than tiny, attainable dreams."

"Tiny and attainable to you. Everest for me." Rory balled her feet up inside of her shoes. She fiddled with the hem of her gray blouse as her mind drifted to the melancholy that always came after these phone calls. Her blouse had a layer of black lace underneath that flared at her hips, and trembled when she was busy hating herself. Her black trousers were wrinkle-free, and her sensible shoes clacked nervously as her knees bobbed up and down. She'd been in meetings all day, but this one phone call grated on her nerves like nothing else could.

"The investors for the playground need to be contacted this week. Is that on my list or yours?"

"Mine." Rory rifled through the stack of papers to find the to-do list she'd lost in the sea of documents. "I'm not thrilled on the commitment from Davin Industrial. They're giving less to the Foundation than they did last year, but asking for more business from us."

"They're capitalists, Rory. That's usually the way of things. But you're right, I didn't anticipate them pledging less. I'll follow up."

"Okay. I'll lean on the Literacy Fellowship to get us their recommended curriculum for next year. They were supposed to have that submitted to us already."

"Francesca was supposed to handle that. The point of having an assistant is that you don't have to do everything."

"She tried, but here we are." Synching their busy

schedules took so long that Rory grew frustrated. "Do you think we work too much?"

Remus offered up a perfunctory laugh. "I think if we didn't, Avondale wouldn't have the things and rights it needs to thrive. You've got the four-thirty staff meeting, right?"

"I'll be five minutes late. I've got that interview with Royal Watch for their piece on me – The Last Days of Aurora Johnstone." Her jaw stiffened every time the title of the countdown article came across her schedule.

Rory wondered when the last time it was that it mattered if she thrived. She recalled the steps that led her to spending her Sundays rifling through papers and contracts with her uncle, and couldn't justify the mess that had grown so out of control that she couldn't grant herself a day off. Her lunch hour had been spent gritting her teeth through the Baron's needling. The last thing she wanted to do was sit down with the national publication and talk about how she was spending her last months serving Avondale.

But she was the future Chancellor, so a luxury such as privacy wasn't something the world was concerned with granting her.

"Rory?" Remus called his niece again, but Rory's mind was far, far away from the office where she'd spent most of her adulthood. The walls of the tall building that was always bustling with activity usually gave her a steady dose of comfort, but now it felt like a coffin.

She'd never gone skydiving.

She'd never even had a vacation by herself.

She'd never... So many things had been put on hold so she could focus on her goal that had always burned white-hot in her chest – make the greatest impact on the world in the short time she was given. Most people didn't know their expiration date, but Rory's had been widely publicized, thanks to the curse she'd received at birth.

The Baron had been right on one thing – there was a timeclock on her days, and it was quickly running out. She'd done all she could to make sure Avondale thrived in her absence when her curse came into effect, while sacrificing perhaps too much of herself.

Remus was right; she'd made her dreams small, so she could fulfill the dreams of others by granting them funding and education through her Foundation. Her life would be put on a permanent pause soon. With the Baron's words still ringing in her ears, she realized she didn't want her life to stop, having never lived it.

"Rory? Are you alright?"

Rory tugged her hair behind her ear and blinked the world around her back into focus with panic lining her eyes.

This wasn't right. How had she ever thought this was a solid life plan? Seventy-hour workweeks ensured she accomplished a lot, but it left her with a hollowness that seemed to be growing larger the closer she got to her twenty-fifth birthday.

She didn't have all the details worked out, but she knew she couldn't continue on another second, keeping things as they were. She moved toward the door with sudden purpose. "Uncle Remus? I think I need to step away."

Though she realized Remus most likely assumed she was going to get some air, Rory knew her feet wouldn't be satisfied until they were running far, far away from the life that used to be her own.

2

RORY JOHNSTONE, THE CRIMINAL

"If only I had a Pulse, breaking and entering would be so much easier."

The teasing voice on the other end of the line tsked her, as if he could see her tripping over the errant roots along the path behind the log cabin. "My, my. Rory Johnstone, what a devious little minx you are."

"If my Pulse was Sweetness, I could cajole the nearest locksmith and get myself inside with a simple touch. Or if my Pulse was Persuasion. But no."

"Your problem isn't that you were born a Deadpulse, but that you ran away without securing the key from me first."

"You sure you can't meet me up here? Come on, Henry. The last time the three of us went on vacation was how many years ago? Three? Four? That's shameful." The bottom of Rory's black ballet flats were sticky from pine tree sap, but that didn't dampen her spirits. She was determined to make the most of her getaway. It was only a matter of time before her guard tracked her down and brought her back home.

"I don't think I can persuade Adam to leave his castle, and sadly, I have actual princely duties to tend to."

"Because you're so very important?" she mocked him with a smile as she climbed the steps onto the dark wood stained deck, plopping her backpack down on the picnic table.

"You joke, but yes. One day when my father hands down his crown to me, and your father hands down his seat on the head of the council to you, then it'll be you and me ruling Avondale. One of us has to be the responsible adult today. As you're the one ditching your guard and running through the woods toward a cabin without a key, I guess that'll have to be me."

Rory balked, flipping her straight black hair over her shoulder. "You know that's usually me! You told me this was a good idea. You're the one who agreed that I was working too much, and needed a break."

"Ah, that's right. I'm so wise. But did I tell you to run off without the key?"

Rory grumbled as she cupped her hands on either side of her face, peering in through the cabin window. "Who doesn't keep a spare key lying around?"

"Um, princes who value their privacy."

She squinted, her lips drawing to the side. "It looks like you redecorated."

"Did I? That's probably true. I haven't had all that much time to get out to the cabin. The last time I was there, I want to say I bought a giant bear rug. Thought it might scare away prowlers. Frightened me enough in the store. However, it doesn't seem to be working on keeping you out, so perhaps I should ask for my money back."

"If the whole prince thing doesn't work out for you, I don't recommend a career in comedy." She cast around for anything she could use to pry open the window. "How mad would you be if I broke the window?"

"Somewhere between hopping and raging."

"Bill me. I'm not going back. Benjamin will be so mad when he realizes I ditched him. One week alone. That's all I wanted."

"And you could've had that. With your guard."

"I feel like you don't understand what 'alone' means."

"I feel like you don't understand what 'breaking and entering' means."

A thrill raced through Rory's veins, curving the corners of her mouth upward. "I've actually never committed a crime before. Breaking and entering? That seems like something I should do, being that it's my last year on earth."

Henry's voice grew grim. "I do wish you'd stop talking like that. Your curse probably won't hold."

Rory was done listening. "Have to go. Committing a

crime." Then she ended the call, searching for the perfect rock that might prove most effective. She didn't want to talk about what hope her few friends and family entertained. She didn't want to weigh in on the gossip websites that kept a running tally of voters chiming in on whether or not Rory Johnstone would prick her finger on a sewing needle on her twenty-fifth birthday and go into a deep sleep, as predicted. True love's kiss was the only antidote that would be able to wake her, but Rory knew that was as good as no cure at all, since she'd never been in love before. Though, her uncle had done his best to counter the curse Malaura had placed on her at birth. A coma was better than death, she supposed.

Four months left, and she had so much more she wanted to experience, so much she wanted to accomplish. Breaking and entering hadn't been on her list before that evening, but suddenly it made its way to top slot. She found a rock next to the deck, welcoming the adrenaline that excited her – made her feel alive. She relished those moments, and knew there wouldn't be many left for her to enjoy.

Rory cranked her arm back and launched the rock at the window, laughing in shock at her daring as the glass shattered. She covered her mouth, gleeful as she bobbed on her toes at the damage.

It wasn't until the alarm sounded that Rory realized what Henry was no doubt calling her back to warn her about. She jumped back from the cabin, fumbling with her phone and shouting into it. "I set off the alarm!"

"You don't say. It's almost as if I don't want people breaking into my homes."

Rory covered her ear, wincing at the sound that pierced the evening stillness. Birds flew away, making Rory feel the need to apologize to them. "What's your alarm code?" When Henry rattled off six digits, she softened, despite the blaring noise. "That's my birthday."

"It is? Well, I'll be. Enjoy your contraband before you're hauled off to my dungeon. I daresay the accommodations are slightly less comfortable there. Though, there's no bearskin rug in the cells, so it's probably not quite as scary."

Rory ended the call and reached her arm in, fumbling with the doorknob. Her fingers slipped twice before she finally turned the latch. She let out a hiss as the glass sliced through her arm. "Oh, ow! Yeah, that stings." She ran into the cabin, trying to remember where the keypad was, finally locating it near the front door. She shrieked at the bearskin rug, but hopped over the head as the alarm blared through the house. It wasn't until she keyed in her own birthday that her shoulders relaxed.

"Oh, that's much better. I can hear myself think." She snatched up a rag from the cupboard in the kitchen and banded it around her forearm to stem the bleeding, looking away from the wound with a wince. She tried not to think about the blood, which always made her a little queasy. Fainting when Henry had cut himself on a can opener when she was eight years old was a thing she'd never lived down. Though she tried to roll her eyes at the teasing, the sight of blood still made her feel woozy.

Once the blood was cleverly hidden beneath the rag, a gust of relief flew out of her. The lack of noise left room for her mind to process the semi-familiar surroundings. She hadn't been to the secret cabin in years, but recalled many a fond memory that took place over the dinner table, on the couch, out by the lake, on the deck, and in the woods.

The brown couch had the faint stink of cigars to it, bringing her back to Adam's brief stint of smoking that her and Henry had protested with much dramatic gagging. Whenever things grew too serious or harrowing, they would retreat to Henry's cabin that Adam had helped him secure. It was one of the perks of being close friends with the son of a real estate mogul. Adam had houses all over Avondale. As the years passed, though, Adam grew more and more agoraphobic, never leaving his castle. With Henry in his palace, Adam in his castle, and Rory in her mansion, luxuries like cabins fell to the wayside. The cabin had been largely untouched in the past few years.

Rory had known the cabin where they'd spent much of their adolescence would be available and quiet. As she looked around, the lack of cameras made her shoulders loosen. There was no one shouting questions at her about things that just plain didn't matter. Yes, she had less than a year left before her curse was due to set in. No, she hadn't found anyone she was in love with. Part of that was due to the press. They wanted their future Chancellor to be healthy, whole and well, so each date she went on was surrounded by cameras, complete with a play-by-play recap of the date the next day online on Royal Watch. They meant well, she guessed, but it only made it harder for her to find anyone.

She brought her backpack up to her bedroom and started putting her clothes in the musty drawers using her non-bloodied arm, wishing the reporters had hounded her to ask the truly important questions. How was her foundation doing? Did they need more volunteers?

She'd made her peace with the impending pause on her life, but felt unrest only for the work that needed to be done for her charity that she wouldn't be able to continue if she was in a coma. Magic was such a concentrated focus in Avondale, so all too often, formal education took a backseat. This made for accomplished Pulse-wielding, but there were large factions of the land that were nearly illiterate because of the lack of focus placed on traditional education. Rory's foundation raised money and put programs in place to balance out the educational gap. Still, the reporters mainly wanted to talk about the superficial things, once again pushing education to the back burner.

Rory tried to ignore the slice in her arm, hoping it would clot and clean and heal itself somehow without her having to look at the blood. Her knees felt weak at the mere thought of what lie beneath the rag, so she leaned back onto the bare mattress, feeling the creak of the springs as her slight body shifted. She stared up at the wooden slats in the ceiling, recalling the many games she'd played with Henry and Adam. Of course, that was years ago, back when Adam had been young and fun, and Henry had been less busy with trying to fill the very big shoes that would one day be handed to him.

She'd been different back then, too. She'd always been driven to make the biggest impact with the limited time she knew she had, but in the past handful of years, that drive had spiked, pushing her schedule to a frenzied pace. Her uncle had teased her that if the curse failed at bringing her down on her twenty-fifth birthday, a heart attack was sure to do the job.

They didn't understand, though. They had their whole lives to make an impact. They had years to waste, time to indulge. She had twenty-five years. A quarter of a century, and that was it. Ever since she'd started the foundation, she was determined to make her light burn bright, no matter how short a time it had to blaze a path for Avondale to follow.

Rory knew her arm would need to be dealt with; she could already feel the blood soaking through the rag. Her parents would need to be called and reassured that she was okay, even though she'd left them a note. They worried so much nowadays. She knew she'd have to deal with Benjamin, who would surely be angry she'd ditched him, making him look unsuitable to guard the Chancellor's daughter.

Rory didn't hear the footsteps until they reached the stairs, creaking beneath the weight of someone who made a far bigger tread than she. She bolted up in the bed, scrambling off it as she clutched her forearm to her chest. Her eyes darted around the room, assessing with immediate despair the lack of items that could be used to fend off the errant attacker. Grabbing up the pillow, she wound back and readied herself to swing at the intruder when he rounded the corner. Fear clutched her around the throat, but she was determined not to panic.

The man didn't give her a chance to fight back before he lunged into the room, spun Rory around, and pinned her to the wooden wall, knocking the breath from her in a gust. "You picked the wrong house to break into. Whatever you think you're about to steal, best put it back now. If you knew whose cabin this was, you wouldn't be in here causing trouble."

Rory struggled fruitlessly against the man's solid form. He was a few inches taller than her, his minty breath tickling her neck in bursts as they both dueled with their adrenaline. "I'm not stealing anything. This is my friend's cabin! Let me go!"

He twisted her good arm behind her, forcing her to drop the pillow. He didn't jerk her around too much or inflict pain, but merely communicated the steadiness of a warning that shenanigans would not be tolerated.

"Friends usually have a key if they're invited to stay at someone's home away from home. You wouldn't have had to break in and set off the alarm if you were invited."

Rory harrumphed, giving another frustrated struggle before she growled out her anger. "Fine, call the police. I appreciate what you're trying to do, but it's really not necessary. We can wait it out, and you'll see that everything's fine."

"Sounds like a solid plan."

Rory felt him reach for his phone, which drew her eyes downward.

She hadn't been expecting the blood. Though she knew she'd been cut, she assumed enough time had passed that her arm would have clotted. The crimson goo dripped down her wrist and slipped between her fingers, turning them clammy as the image emblazoned itself in her brain. "Oh, no." Her breathing grew shallow, and suddenly the man who was holding her against the wall wasn't just keeping her in place. The stranger scrambled to hold Rory upright when her knees turned to jelly.

She hadn't fainted in so long. Each time brought about a panic from her parents, thinking she was slipping into her coma before the doomed time.

But her parents weren't there, only a stranger she didn't know, whom she was trusting could catch her. She knew she should look away from the sight, but her eyes couldn't tear themselves from the puddle that was gathering on the wood floor, marking this spot with her DNA.

Her initials were carved into the bunk beds in the next room that Henry and Adam used to share, but this spot was now hers alone, stained with... with...

Rory tried not to cry out when her legs collapsed beneath her. She tried not to give in to the darkness that hedged in the edges of her vision. "Don't let me... I can't... The blood..."

The light faded from view, and finally Rory's body gave in to the crash.

3

NEW NEIGHBOR

Rory awoke to a cold compress on her forehead, and a thumb gently caressing the back of her hand. "Henry?" She opened her eyes, but immediately regretted the feat of grandeur. Her vision swam, coaxing a groan from her lips.

"Easy, now. It's all fine."

She didn't recognize the voice, but the low cadence soothed her. For the moment, she trusted in the sweetness that held onto her limp hand. She couldn't feel skin, but realized the man was wearing gloves.

Her second attempt at opening her eyes went slightly better, taking only a handful of blinks to bring the world into focus. The light was on in the bedroom, making up for the fact that the sun was setting outside, and filtering in a faint glow that touched on the man who was still holding onto her hand. "How did I..."

"I didn't mean to make you faint. I thought you were breaking and entering. Then when you passed out, I got a good look at you. I didn't realize who you were."

Rory's mouth was dry, her tongue working overtime to unstick itself from the roof of her mouth. "How'd you get in here?"

He glanced right and then left, as if she'd asked him a trick question. "Um, through the window in the door you broke? The alarm went off, so I ran on over. I own the cabin next door."

Rory's nose scrunched, trying to think of meeting any neighbors before, but none came to mind. "Next door?"

The man jerked his gloved hand to the right. "I own the property that way. Met Prince Henry a couple times. He's a nice enough guy, so I keep an eye on his cabin whenever something like this comes up."

"That's thoughtful of you." She meant to rub her forehead, but accidentally slapped herself across the face, groaning at the mess of it all.

The man chuckled at her plight. "Is that what you meant to do, your grace?"

Rory sighed, wishing she wasn't making a complete fool of herself. "I forgot to get the key from Henry. I didn't mean to set off the alarm. I just wanted some peace and quiet."

The man raised his eyebrow at her. He had dark skin that captivated Rory with its handsomeness. His long lashes and unassuming brown eyes drew her in as he spoke. "I'm not sure you're nailing the 'quiet' part. That's the loudest security alarm I've ever heard."

Rory laughed through her nose. "Yeah, our friend owns a security company on the side. I probably should've called him first to let him know I was breaking in."

"You really are just a terrible burglar." Using a bit of magic, he levitated the cloth from her forehead, and moved it over to the nightstand. Then he coiled an arm under her shoulders, taking care to move her slowly to a sitting position. "Easy, now." He leaned her up against the headboard, his gloved hands gentle with her body.

It wasn't until then that Rory realized her arm was bandaged up, concealing the cut from view. "Oh, you fixed my arm! Thank you. I cut it when I was breaking in. The sight of blood makes me queasy. That's why I fainted."

His sculpted lips pulled to the side, making him look like he was trying to be diplomatic through her plight, holding back a laugh. "That's quite the predicament. Here, drink some water." He molded her fingers around a sealed bottle, unscrewing it for her before he helped her bring it to her lips.

Rory swallowed down her chagrin, taking gulps that cleared her mind so she could fully appreciate the man's kind eyes that were filled with humility. He was muscular, but not overly tall. He wore a gray long-sleeved shirt paired with jeans and sturdy boots. As he watched her fiddle with the label on the bottle, she noticed a few objects from her bag floating in the air behind him, as if he couldn't help but levitate things when he was thinking about something. Her uncle sometimes did that without meaning to, but Remus Johnstone was one of the most powerful magic-wielders of their time.

"What's your name?" she asked.

"Cord." Then he cleared his throat, as if reminding himself of his manners. "Cordray Phillips. And you're Aurora Johnstone."

"Rory," she corrected him. "Aurora is what the papers call me. You've seen me pass out. I think we're beyond formalities."

He ran his hands down the front of his shirt and glanced around the bedroom. "Should I call your fiancé? Let him know you're alright?"

Her nose scrunched as she set the closed water bottle on the mattress at her side. "Who?"

"Prince Henry. I saw the pictures of his proposal. Congratulations."

Rory's eyes cast up to the ceiling, wishing she could shake her head at Henry in person. "He's always doing that to get a rise out of me. We're not engaged. We've never even dated. He just likes to put on a show for the reporters when they won't leave us alone."

Cordray's eyebrows shot up. "Wow. Well, that's quite the show. I've never proposed to a woman as a joke before."

"Good. Women hate that. Can you hand me my phone?"

He shook his head as if to teasingly scold her for the scandal. "Rory, Rory, what's your story?"

She leaned back against the headboard, flexing her fingers to make sure everything felt in good working order. "I was hoping my story would be absolutely nothing for the next week or so. It's hard for me to get away, and then when I finally do, I scare all the woodland creatures for a mile."

He sniggered at the media circus that had delighted in their engagement. Though, there had been many tall tales of the two getting engaged, then breaking up, then getting engaged, then calling it off.

Cordray scooped her phone up off the dresser and pressed it into her palm. "I admit, you two definitely put on a good show for the viewers. I'm pretty well tucked away from the hustle and bustle, but even I heard about that one."

"You live out here? Like, not just coming to the woods for an escape every now and then?"

He leaned back in the wooden chair, balancing on two legs with his boots on the frame of her bed to keep himself steady. "Four years out here. I go into the city every now and then to get supplies and catch up on the latest 'who's marrying whom' gossip, but maybe I should've just stuck to refilling my cupboards."

"Always a safe bet. It's nice out here."

"Despite the occasional breaking and entering, yes. It's quiet. Not a whole lot of nonsense. People tend to leave each other alone. I guess that's probably why you came to stay here."

Rory nodded her head as she put in a call to her favorite prince. "Hey, Henry. I got in. I'll have the window replaced before I leave."

Henry groaned. "You broke a window? Are you alright?"

"I'm fine. Your neighbor actually helped bandage me up. Cordray says hello."

Cord bowed his head with a relaxed smile, his hands folded over his stomach.

Henry's voice grew grim. "Rory, be careful with him."

Rory's spine stiffened. "What do you mean?"

"Cordray's a nice guy. Great to have as a neighbor for a property I hardly visit. But don't let him too near you. There's a reason he lives out in the woods."

Rory's gaze flicked over to Cord. She could tell he could hear Henry's warning by the hardening of his eyes that stared out the window as he rocked his chair back and forth on its two legs. The objects floating behind him in the air now seemed menacing, instead of playful.

"Henry?" she said, breathless as her palms began to sweat.

The prince's voice came back with a swift verdict. "Cordray Phillips is a Lethal."

4

ROBBING A BANK

When Rory ended the call, she tried to keep her demeanor light, but her voice came out squeaky and pinched. "You've lived out here four years, you said? That's nice."

Cordray set all four legs down on the wooden floor with a bang, leaning forward so he could rest his elbows on his thighs and level his gaze at her. "And there it is."

Rory brought her knees up and wrapped her arms around her shins. Protecting her body was a futile attempt when going up against a Lethal, but she couldn't help the fear that drove her closer to fight-or-flight mode. "There *what* is?"

He jabbed his gloved finger at her with an even tone that was laced with accusation. "The government claims they care about the Lethals, but you're just as afraid as everyone else. We're guilty before we have a chance to prove ourselves."

Rory's mouth hung open, momentarily forgetting about the cut on her arm. "That's really what you think? How would you expect someone to react when they're in a room with a person who could murder them with a single touch?"

"I would expect any sane, compassionate person to thank the man who took care of you while you were passed out, bandaged your arm, brought you water, and sat with you until you felt better. Lethals are great for enforcing security, but apparently not much else."

"Cordray, I didn't mean anything by..."

He stood, a look of sheer disappointment on his face. "I expect this of Avondale's citizens. They only know what the papers tell them. Malaura is rumored to be gathering up her Lethals, gearing up for some unknown nefarious attack. It's all so scary to them. But you? You're in the exact same position I am."

Rory's eyebrow quirked in confusion. "What position is that?"

He gestured around the mildly furnished cabin. "One where you have to resort to hiding out in the woods to get some peace and quiet. One where people read something online and make assumptions about your entire life and who you are." He moved to stand in the doorway, his voice quieting as he glared at her. "One where people judge your usefulness based on your Pulse."

Rory bristled, draping her legs over the edge of the bed as she rolled her shoulders back. "Is that supposed to be a crack at me because I'm a Deadpulse? Am I somehow less because I can't perform even the most basic spells?"

He gripped the doorjamb with one hand and pointed in her face with the other. "The thing is, I never cared about any of that. Of all people, I know that a person's Pulse doesn't define them; it's what they do with their whole life that makes them a monster or a man." He banged his fist to his chest. "I am not a monster!"

When he made to leave, Rory called out for forgiveness. "Cord, wait!" She tried to get up to plead with him, to make him understand the stigma (as if he didn't already). But the moment she stood, she realized her mistake too late. Her legs weren't sturdy enough to support her yet, and her knees buckled, plummeting her downward toward the wooden floor.

Cordray swore as he darted forward to catch her, his arms scooping her up before she hit the ground, her legs dangling over his forearm. Their hearts beat quickly as the frenzy of their fight crackled in the air around them, but as the seconds wore on, Rory errantly wondered when the last time was that she'd been figuratively swept off her feet. Academically, she knew he was dangerous, but the genuine hurt in his eyes pinged at the more subtle parts of her. There was a gentleness to his steady movements that brought trust to the surface, when normally she'd been instructed to retreat from someone so deadly. Without understanding every nuance, being held in his sturdy arms helped her stiff limbs begin to relax.

She didn't mean to lean her head against the meat of his shoulder, just as she was sure Cordray didn't mean to rest his chin atop her head. Possibility crackled in the air around them, and before she could stop herself, her hand found its way to his neck. Her fingers traced the slope from his shoulder up to the edge of his jaw, just so she could acquaint herself with the feel of his skin.

Just as soon as she felt his shiver under the care of her touch, she withdrew her fingers, suddenly embarrassed. "I'm sorry. I..."

"Easy," he whispered, and then gently deposited her atop the mattress, fluffing the pillows around her as she leaned her spine against the headboard. There was a hard edge to his eyes, and Rory could see he was making a concerted effort not to touch her, so as not to spook her. When he took a step back from the bed, he raised his hands to prove their innocence. "See? I won't hurt you. You can see I'm wearing my gloves. You know you can't Pulse another person if your hands are covered."

In the room that was clean, with sheets tailored to her affinity for grays with a lavender accent, Rory felt like the ball of chaos that didn't belong in the space. She'd broken a window, fainted, and insulted a perfectly decent man who went above and beyond to look out for Henry's interests.

Rory rubbed her knuckles into her forehead. "I was

completely off the mark. I'm sorry, Cord. We do so much talk about what to do with the Lethals, making sure policies are fair to them, but I'm not actually allowed to be too near them."

Cordray's eyes lifted to the ceiling, as if reining his indignation in so he didn't devolve into fruitless arguing. "To your credit, I actually think the king and your father's policies on equal rights for Lethals are decent. But you can't preach about tolerance if you recoil every time you're around one of us."

Rory frowned at him, her bout of wooziness taking away much of her tact. "All due respect, but I can feel as wary as I want around a Lethal. I've been abducted eight times, and each of those instances involved Lethals."

"Eight times?" His shoulders deflated, and the fight seemed to go out of him. His gaze softened as it landed on her. "Jeez. I didn't know that."

"Not many people do. My parents keep as much as they can away from the press. If it leaks out that a Lethal is causing problems, it could turn into a witch hunt, and all our hard work at getting equal rights for your kind will go out the door." She took a chance and motioned for him to sit on the mattress near her feet. "Still, *you* didn't abduct me. I shouldn't have reacted like that."

Cordray tugged on her toe, giving her a playful smile as a peace offering. "Forgiven. You feeling alright? Almost ready to set off on your next criminal activity?"

"I'm thinking I should rob a bank next. I'm far better at

stealth than I imagined." She held up her bandaged arm with a crooked smile.

"Just a bank? I think we should go bigger. Something with an even louder alarm system. Go big or go home, right?"

Cordray kept an eye on the door while they planned out their imaginary heist, as if he expected to have to ward off intruders from snatching at the Chancellor's daughter. The two laughed as they drew fictional floorplans of various high-profile buildings they would break into together, their fingers tracing escape routes into the comforter between them. As the minutes ticked by, Rory realized how very easy it was to relax around Cordray. He asked thoughtful questions about which monuments they would vandalize and why, and when would be the best time of year, so no devious behavior coincided with important things, like National Jam Day.

Sure, she joked around with Henry, Remus, and occasionally Adam. This felt different. Cordray smelled like freshly sawed pine and laundry detergent. His muscles were thick, no doubt from outdoor labor. There was a quiet calm to him that permitted her heart to flutter without judgment while she worked through exactly why she hadn't pulled away from him yet. It wasn't an everyday occurrence a man sat on her bed, but the sight burned in her vision in ways that reminded her she was on vacation, which was when scandalous things could be entertained.

When she sneezed from the dust, Cordray got up and

opened the window to let in a gust of the crisp air. "Oh, that's wonderful. It doesn't smell like this in the city."

Cordray drew in a long breath with a look of contentment as he gazed out the window. "That's one of the perks of living out here."

He was a sight to behold against the sunlight that streamed in to highlight his sharp cheekbones, the sensual curves of his upper lip, and the firmness of his chest that Rory studied with perhaps too much fascination. When he'd lifted her off the ground to keep her from falling, something chaotic in her calmed when her body rested against his chest. She'd felt the inner angst of her impending life's pause begin to quiet to a deep sigh she'd been hoping her vacation would produce.

Yet, it wasn't nature, nor was it the lovely cabin that was outfitted for such escapes. It was his arms that quieted her spinning schedule and the fear that was always looming that she wouldn't accomplish enough – wouldn't *be* enough – before she was no more.

Before she knew what she was doing, Rory was out of the bed and by his side at the window, feeling oddly settled the closer she got to him. She knew she should be nervous about his Lethal magic, and part of her was, but she didn't worry for her safety any longer. Instead of anxiety, it was butterflies that batted around in her belly, quickening her heartrate as she breathed in the earthy scent of him. "Is that why you live out here? Because you're Lethal?"

Cordray glanced down at her, his body shifting so it was more open to her – inviting without touching. "Let's not bog it all down with things we both know will be hard to talk about. A cabin in the woods is a good option for me. It's peaceful, uncomplicated, and every now and then I get to stop a beautiful prowler. Don't go feeling sorry for me, Story. This is a good life for someone like me."

The corner of her mouth twitched. "Story?"

His neck shrank almost impishly, and he looked back out the window to avoid her gaze. "Yeah. Everyone has a story about you, but it doesn't seem like the real one gets to come out all that often."

She tucked a lock of hair behind her ear, her cheeks rounding with the hint of a smile. "I like that."

His chest rounded out as he reached forward, as if to place his hand on her hip, but then suddenly withdrew it. His eyes widened, as if she was the one who was danger-ous, and touching her would lend itself to certain doom.

Though she knew all the reasons why she shouldn't, Rory couldn't help herself. Her hand moved of its own accord to rest on his chest. She thrilled at the brazen act, wondering if this was the rush the rest of the world got to glory in. Now it was her turn, and she wasn't about to back away from the heady addiction that was rapidly taking hold of her.

She felt him shudder, as if the flutter of her fingers had been sensual in nature.

"Sorry," he said as he cleared his throat. "Not too many

people are brave enough to touch a Lethal. It's... That's..." He drew in a steadying breath, his hand moving to cover hers, keeping it there so she could feel the rapid jumps of his heart. "This is the best break-in I've ever been to."

Rory knew she should pull her hand from his chest, but the muscles were so firm – his heartbeat so pure. For such a complicated situation, being near him felt unbelievably simple. Her life had been mired by too many decisions, too much controversy. To have a moment of uninterrupted sweetness made her want to live in the warmth of his touch, deadly though it was.

"I don't know what I'm doing," she admitted in a whisper, alarmed at how brazen she was behaving.

Cordray caught her wrist, his voice turning husky with a low note of desire. "I do." His other arm coiled around her hips with the promise of better things to come.

When her phone rang, they both jolted with the suddenness of the interruption. Rory jumped back, her hand flying to her forehead as it dawned on her how out of character she was behaving. Cordray shook his head as if trying to rid himself of the haze in which they both found themselves mired.

Rory fished around on the bed for her cell phone, sighing when she saw who was calling. "I'm sorry. I have to take this." She answered with practiced patience. "Hi, Benjamin."

"Is there a reason you've decided to go completely off-book today? You told me you were going to lie down."

"I was just doing exactly that. I didn't mention where I would be napping, so technically, not a lie."

"That had better be your idea of a joke. I've been looking everywhere for you!"

She cringed at Benjamin's seething. She could picture his brown hair slightly tousled from his harried search for her, and the crease between his eyebrows when he'd no doubt found her note. He was twenty years her senior, and she'd always thought of him as an uncle. Guilt washed through her at having worried him, though she knew she couldn't have granted herself this time alone if she hadn't cut and run when she did. "I left you a note."

"Do you want me to call you 'young lady'? Because I will if you don't march yourself back here in the next ten seconds."

Rory cast Cordray a look of apology when he made his way to the door. He met her eyes with a softness to his smile that told her he'd enjoyed their brief time together as much as she had.

Only she realized she didn't want anything about their interaction to be brief. She craved buckets and buckets of experiences with him, bathing in nothing but time, which always seemed to be slipping through her fingers. How she wanted to hold onto him.

Rory reached out and grabbed onto his fingers, surprising them both with her daring. Though his hands were gloved, it was only a thin layer of fabric that kept him from killing her by accident. No one touched Lethals, for fear of being errantly murdered or put in the hospital.

Cordray stopped his exit, standing stock-still in the doorway just to prolong the simple touch. It breathed humaneness into them both, reminding them that though their worlds involved a fair amount of ostracism, there was still tenderness and closeness to be discovered.

"I'm not in the area, Benjamin. But I'm safe, I promise."

"Oh, that makes me feel so much better. You're not safe unless I'm there, because it's my job to make sure you're not taken again. You realize that your twenty-fifth birthday is coming up, right? Malaura isn't going to trust her curse to hold. She'll want to be up close to make sure it unfolds exactly as she designed it. This isn't the time to run off!"

Rory wanted to shout at him, but kept her decorum as much as one might expect from a politician's daughter. "Either way, I'm going to fall into my coma. No matter if I'm with you or far away. You can't protect me, Benjamin. I've got four months left, and I want to spend a little of my time by myself." She gripped the phone, wishing she wasn't having this conversation in front of the newcomer, yet she was unwilling to let go of Cordray's hand. "I'll check in by phone every night and each morning. Henry knows where I'm at, and that I'm safe."

She could tell that her guard was trying to rein in his temper. "Rory, I swear."

"Love you, too, and I'll talk to you in the morning." She could scarcely believe her daring when she ended the call, staring at her phone in wonder. "I can't believe I just did that."

Cordray squeezed her fingers, studying their joined hands with wonder. "It was pretty incredible."

As if only just realizing what her hand was doing, Rory retracted her reach, her neck shrinking with chagrin. "I'm sorry. I know I don't know you. I'm not usually so... I'm all turned around."

Cordray shoved his hands into his pockets, a bashful smirk toying at the edges of his lips. "A beautiful woman who can't stop holding my hand is never a bad thing." He held her gaze, tearing it away when her phone rang again. "I should probably go. Your guard probably wouldn't be too thrilled to know you're in a cabin alone with a Lethal." He didn't say it in a self-pitying way, but with a firm commitment to her safety and peace of mind.

She made to argue, but when she glanced at the phone and saw the number, she grimaced. "Actually, it's my parents. I should probably take this."

He bowed his head to her. "Take care, Story."

Her fingers made to reach for him again, but she stopped herself short, and then stared at her hand, as if to ask it just what it thought it was doing.

"Hello, Mom," she said as Cordray disappeared into the hallway. Her mother filled her ear with fretting, but she only heard the boots of Cordray as he tromped down the steps and moved out of the cabin into the woods.

5

TERRIBLE AT VACATIONS

The sun filtered through the edges of the curtains when morning finally roused Rory. She yawned, stretching like a cat atop the mattress. Her throat was scratchy from the outdoors, but she couldn't remember having slept so well in months. She'd turned her phone off – actually off – before she'd gone to sleep. The relief of no one being able to contact her was a restfulness she felt deep down in her bones.

Rory set about her morning taking her time with the little things indulging in an extra long shower, forgoing the need for coffee as she let her body wake up on its own, and doing yoga as she let her hair air-dry in the living room. She hadn't had the time to read for fun in ages, and had packed a few books from the family's study that she cracked open with gusto. She knew there was much to see to with her foundation, but she'd hired an assistant for this very reason. Francesca was supposed to be taking things off her plate so she could have the occasional day off. She'd left Francesca a to-do list, but wasn't sure the woman was capable of staying on top of everything just yet. The night before she'd ditched and ran, she'd left her uncle Remus a list, as well. Though she knew he would understand her need for respite, she regretted not telling him about her escape to his face.

Rory read four chapters of a historical romance novel before the lure of work proved too strong to resist. She opened her backpack and spread out the folders and files that most needed her attention. She knew there was no internet out in the cabin, and loved it for that luxury, but there was still work to be done. She ignored the many texts and phone calls when she powered up her cell, calling only Remus to assure him she was alright.

"You should've told me you needed a break," he scolded her.

"I'm not sure either of us would've heard me. I'll be back in a week. I'm still working on drafting up the proposal for the new playground. Francesca should be able to handle most of the things on my daily checklist."

"I want you to listen to the words you just said. There's no way Francesca can handle your job – yet or ever."

"Well, in four months, I'll be gone for good. Best she gets the hang of things now."

Rory hadn't meant to bring the phone call to a crashing halt, but the silence rang of discomfort all the same. "We'll find a way to wake you up," Remus promised, not for the first time.

"Mm-hm. Could you do me a favor and let my parents and Benjamin know I'm fine? Mom and Dad seemed alright with it after I reasoned with them last night, but I couldn't talk Benjamin down."

"Sure, give me the impossible job. Your father's right here, by the way. Whatever version of 'alright' you think your parents are right now, they're not."

Rory softened at the sound of her father's voice as he took the phone from his younger brother. "I knew you'd call Remus first. Are you okay, sweetheart?"

"I'm perfectly fine. Just taking a little vacation. I'm twenty-four, and I've never had a trip by myself. Thought it was about time."

She could tell her father wanted to argue, but couldn't very well force his grown daughter to march herself on home. "Okay, Rory. If you say you need this, then I can respect that. I wish you'd taken Benjamin. The man's driving himself insane going to all your usual haunts."

"Tell Benjamin I love him, and to put his feet up and enjoy the week off."

Her father's tone came back dubious. "I feel as if we're talking about two different people. This is Benjamin. A week off to him would be torture."

"I love you, Dad. I'm turning my phone off now."

True to her word, Rory powered down her phone and smiled at the rebellion. Though most women her age didn't have such restrictions, those women didn't have a whole country to consider.

It wasn't long before she was elbow-deep in proposals and papers, sifting through contracts and making notes as to who needed to be contacted when she returned.

So deep in thought was she that when a knock sounded at the front door, she nearly jumped out of her skin. She hadn't made a plan for what to do if someone knocked. She didn't know if she should answer, or if pretending no one was home would be more prudent. She settled for peeking through the curtain, a smile lighting her features when she saw who it was.

"Cordray?" She flung open the door, a smile beaming off her face. "It's good to see you."

He was holding a toolbox and looked as if he'd had something prepared to say, but it escaped him at the sight of her. "I just came by to... And I thought..." A wide grin broke out across his face at his stammering. "Good morning, Story. Just came by to see if you needed help with the window."

"That's nice of you. Come on in." Her heartrate picked up as she ushered him inside and locked the door behind them.

He eyed the table as they walked past the dining room toward the kitchen. "What's all that?"

"Oh, just work. It's hard to step away."

He quirked his eyebrow at her. "I don't think you understand vacation."

Rory's mouth drew to the side as it dawned on her that he might have a point. "Well, I can't actually ditch on my responsibilities."

"You can't take a vacation?" He set his toolbox down by the backdoor and came to stand next to her, eyeing the stacks of paperwork. "You run the Johnstone Foundation, right?"

Rory nodded. "Yes. I love the work, but there are a lot of moving parts."

"What are you going to do when..." His eyes cut to her, and then tore away with a flinch. "I'm sorry. You don't need to talk about that."

Rory was well-practiced in the art of talking about her impending pause, which might as well be permanent at this point. She swallowed involuntarily, as she always did when she compartmentalized the thing that would scare her into a therapist's office if she let it. She touched her thumb to each of her fingers, making sure to keep her tone light. "I have an assistant who's supposed to help Uncle Remus after I fall into my sleep. She's new, though, and it's a lot of responsibility to hand over."

"How new?"

Rory grimaced. "Two years."

Cordray paused, giving Rory time to consider what she'd just said.

Her hand rubbed out a wrinkle of worry that etched itself into her forehead. "Maybe Francesca's not so new. I just know that she can't handle everything yet."

"When will she be able to?"

Rory stiffened, her chin jerking up with a note of defiance. "I built this foundation from the ground up. If there was something I needed help with, I would ask."

Cordray tilted his chin in her direction, crossing his arms over his thick chest. He didn't speak, but again let her words sink in so she could digest them and examine their falsity.

Rory's boldness faded, and her shoulders fell. "Okay, maybe that's not entirely true. Maybe Uncle Remus made me get an assistant because I was supposed to start handing things over. But the idea of giving up on my life's work kills me." Her voice quieted, but was no less stubborn. "It's not my time to die yet."

"Is that what you think you're doing by delegating? Are you giving up? Or are you doing what's best for the Johnstone Foundation, even when it cuts into your pride?"

Rory stammered as she took a step back, wanting to find some grounds to refute his logic. "You can't just... You don't know how..." When the right words didn't come to her, she leveled her finger in his face and argued, "You don't get to know me this well!"

The two froze, perplexed at her words, until they both started to chuckle slowly at the strangeness.

Cordray held up his hands. "I admit, I don't know much about you at all. I could be entirely wrong. Who knows?" He motioned to the cluttered table. "Maybe it's me who's been doing vacations all wrong my whole life. This workload looks totally relaxing."

Leaning against the table, Rory's fist balanced on her hip. "Alright, smart guy. Educate me. How do people take vacations?"

"Boy, are you going to be sorry you asked me that."

A slow smile that started at his core climbed throughout his body and lit his features in ways that made Rory want to say something clever to keep that look on his face at all times. His eyes were captivating, holding nothing back from her. His lips had a suppleness to the sculpted look of them. Rory saw herself closing the gap between them just so she could taste his lower lip. In her mind's eye, she saw her lashes flutter, and envisioned his arm around her hips, relishing her one moment of daring.

She took a step back, shaking her head to clear it of the lusty fog she was unaccustomed to. It was then she realized that Cordray had his hand outstretched to her in invitation, and she was shaking her head and moving away.

Still, he kept the gloved invitation extended, a look of tender pleading in his eyes. She couldn't tell if he was pleading on her behalf – wanting to really help her indulge in a life of relaxation, or if he was asking more for himself – wanting to run away with her.

"What do you say, Story?"

It was the sound of his low baritone that drew her in, pushing her hesitations to the side so she could finally place her hand in his. The connection that zinged through her body sent a thrill into her heart, lifting her to stand on the balls of her feet.

With excitement that pushed both of them into giddy grins of scandal, Cordray pulled her out the back door, their feet quickening as they ran out into the beauty and possibility of the woods.

6

RUNNING THROUGH THE WOODS

"**W**here are we going?"

"Away!"

Rory's eyes were wide as she ran alongside him, giggling as they skipped over roots and darted around trees, still attached at the hand and unwilling to let go of each other. Rory thrilled at holding the hand of a man. For something so simple, it was an intimate act for a woman whose life was usually so very guarded.

For Cordray, touch in general was a thing to celebrate. The moment his admission of having a Lethal Pulse came out in conversation, people visibly backed away from him. Though they could have dropped their grip on each other minutes ago, both of them clung tighter, savoring the scandal that was precious to them both.

They ran through the woods, brushing off their burdens in the branches. So much of Rory's life had been spent serving the people and helping the throne. The greens and the browns were lush with the freedom of nature permitting them to run wild, even if mankind never would allow such scandals.

As they moved deeper into the woods, Rory was amazed at how lavishly the forest liked to show off. The trees grew ever taller the further in they went. Summer was just beginning, introducing flowers to the world that not many would have the good fortune to see, but there they bloomed in beautiful bursts of fragrant blues and pinks. The scent of lilacs permeated her nose with a perfume that felt almost spiritual as it filled her lungs to nearly bursting.

It wasn't until they approached a stream that their sprint slowed into a breathy stroll. "I haven't run that long in ages!" She rested her free hand to her chest to quell the rapid jumps. She expected him to release her hand; she knew she was clinging perhaps a little too much. But Cordray never dropped her grip, instead using the tether to draw her closer, so their hips occasionally bumped as they hiked along the trickling brook.

"I love this stretch of the woods. The stream goes all the way down there, and the view is amazing. I think your vacation should start off with a nature hike, not loads of paperwork."

"You're the boss."

"Actually, *you're* the boss. I know I was probably being a little too flippant back there. I know you've got an important job, and you do a lot of amazing things with the work your Foundation does." He shrugged, letting their hands swing between them as they walked along the brook. "There was just something about seeing the hope in your eyes yesterday when you were talking about your big moment of freedom, and then seeing you today chaining yourself when there was finally no one to tether you to a desk. It made me sad." He motioned around the woods. "This is what it looks like when I snap."

Rory's smile felt so permanent at this point; she wondered when the last time was that she'd been so enthralled. "When I snap, it involves working until the candle goes out, and falling asleep at my desk."

"You work by candlelight?"

"After nine, yes. Benjamin, my guard, lights a candle that burns for about three hours. The rule is that I can work until the candle goes out, and then I have to turn in."

"That's oddly sweet."

"Well, that's Benjamin for you. It was Remus' idea, actually. He got tired of me drinking espresso all day at the office. Apparently I can be something of a dictator when most of my dict consists of caffeine."

When they came to a particularly muddy patch, Cordray steered them around it and pointed to the animal tracks. "See that? It's a deer heading south. We'll probably start to see a lot more tracks like that the further in we get."

"Are you a hunter?"

Cordray chuckled. "I'm a vegetarian. Growing up as a Lethal gave me a bent for not killing things."

Rory mulled over his response as they walked through the dewy grass.

"Was that too much melodrama?" he asked, casting her a sidelong glance.

Rory squeezed his fingers twice. "Just the right amount. It's not a chore to learn about you, Cord."

His feet slowed until finally they stopped in front of a felled tree. Instead of hefting one of his legs over the thick trunk, he stared at it, as if perplexed. "No one's ever said that to me. They find out I'm Lethal, and that's all they need to know."

Rory didn't mean to brush the outside of her arm against his, but her body did what it craved without needing to be commanded to move nearer to the man who made her wonder. Instead of speaking, she reached across her body and ran her fingers slowly up and down his forearm, giving them both a steady dose of the shivers.

The mild pop and swish of the water hitting the felled tree drew her eyes, and something about the sight gave her a deep-rooted peace she hadn't been able to access in her office. The air was cleaner out here, the atmosphere still, yet cracking with life. She could feel the chaos that usually banged around inside of her die down under the gentle command of the brook.

Then suddenly, Cordray was several feet away from her, backing up in alarm as if she was the danger, and he, the hunted. "I don't know what this is. I'm not... Why would someone like you be touching me like that? Is this some 'stick it to the parents' thing? Because I've got news for you; I've been that guy before, and I'm not up for it again. Especially not on your family's level. I've got a feeling the Chancellor of Avondale has plenty of obscure places he could use to make me disappear."

Rory took in his worry, and then looked down at her hands, turning them over to examine what made them think they could go off perusing the body of a man she barely knew. "I'm sorry. I shouldn't have been so clingy. It's got nothing to do with 'sticking it to my parents'. I forgot myself for a moment. It won't happen again."

Her words sunk deep in her stomach. For the span of half an hour, she'd completely forgotten about all of her hang-ups. She'd forgotten about work. She'd even forgotten about her curse. So much of her life had been molded around the worst day of her existence. To live without that weight, even for less than an hour, made her giddy with bravery that went beyond reason. She was finally breaking out of her shell and routine enough to realize her life wasn't over yet. She had choices, and she'd never used that liberty to its full capacity.

Her shoulders weighted with a flood of shame, her hands clasping in front as they often did when she was under public scrutiny. She wanted to fidget, but knew that would be eaten up by the press as a weakness. She glanced around the forest that had felt so incredibly alive with freedom mere seconds ago. She scolded herself for believing she belonged there, instead of at her desk, doing what she could to save Avondale, while knowing that it couldn't save her.

Cordray's mistrust was evident in his shifting gaze, but upon taking in her obvious embarrassment, he quickly diverted to compassion. "Hey, I was wrong. I'm the one who should be sorry. I'm not used to nice moments like this that don't have layers and layers of manipulation behind them. This is all me, not you."

Rory lowered her chin and plastered a bland, pleasant expression on her face. She'd worn it on several occasions, and kept it tucked in her back pocket to cover her true face whenever it threatened to come out and expose her pangs of vulnerability. "I should get back. I've ignored my work for far too long. Thank you for the tour."

He recoiled, causing her to stop her exit short. "What is that face?"

Rory flinched. "What?"

"I mean, I've seen you in the papers, and I guess that's how you look, but to see it up close? You were just laughing and smiling, and now you're... I don't know what that is, but it's not you."

"Am I being rude?"

"No."

"I had a lovely walk through the woods, but I let my imagination run away with me. I'm sure my investors wouldn't approve of the childish fantasies I wasted time on when I could have been doing something meaningful."

"What do you know about wasting time? It seems like you've got every second planned out."

A fire flared up in Rory, and for once, she didn't stamp it out with a controlled downward tilt of her head. "Every second that I waste is one I'll never get back. You've got an entire lifetime of seconds – whole minutes and hours and days where you can hide in the woods and trust that the world will find a way to fix itself. I've never had that luxury. I have four months left to solve an entire country's worth of problems. I don't know why I thought it would be a good idea to traipse around the woods like... like..."

"Like what?" Cordray challenged, fanning the flames in her words to keep her true self at the surface as long as possible.

"Like I have a choice in my life!"

"What you have isn't a life!" he countered, his volume climbing. "What you have is a pit that will never fill up, no matter how much dirt you shovel in. You have four months left? Then maybe it's time you started living!"

"You don't know the first thing about me!"

Cordray's voice lowered to almost a whisper. "I know that I felt something, and that doesn't happen for people like me."

Rory threw her arms out, exasperated. "Then why push me away and make me question what was just as special a moment for me?"

Cordray ran his hand from his forehead down his face, his eyes stormy for too many reasons. "Because neither of us has any business pretending that you belong on the arm of a hermit who lives alone in the woods. I could kill you with a single touch."

"You want to talk about me finally living, and then tell me you're too afraid to do the same?"

The two stared at each other for several weighted seconds, soaking in the frustration, vulnerability, and finally, the attraction they couldn't deny any longer.

Rory knew she could run back to the cabin and return to the work she'd set out to tackle on her break from the world. She knew she could cut the whole vacation short and drive home that very afternoon, heading back to what was predictable.

She didn't know what it would be like to kiss Cordray, or what his bottom lip would taste like when she sucked on it.

It took three of her strides to clear the gap between them, her arms coiling around his shoulders as she found herself swept up in his embrace. She scarcely understood her actions, but the tethered girl inside of her slowly became unraveled as her lips captured his. For once, she didn't hold herself back, but took his bleats of attraction mingled with distress, and held them captive in her heart.

7

LIFE WITH CORDRAY

The afternoon slipped by in a haze of frenzied kisses that were followed up by hushed confessions during their unhurried stroll through the woods. There were too many things they wanted to understand about each other for one day together to suffice, but still they did a valiant attempt to cram as much connection as possible into the sunlit hours. It wasn't until their stomachs couldn't be ignored any longer that they headed back to her cabin.

Cordray's gloved hand never left Rory's, as if the twin souls had decided they'd been separated long enough and wouldn't tolerate another minute of division. He squeezed her hand twice to comfort the anxiety that started to spike when they strolled back into her cabin, and she took in the work that had gone unattended to for the entire day.

He motioned to the table. "Don't go here in your mind

yet. Diving right back into a problem situation without clarity isn't going to do you any good."

A worry line creased her forehead, and she bit down on her lower lip. "I can't just duck out on my responsibilities. That's not me."

"Clearly. But if you've got four months left, then maybe you're working on the wrong things. Training your team might be the better move here." He sifted through her mess and lifted a pen out of the piles. "Come to my place. I can help you with this."

Her eyebrow rose as a smirk teased her lips. "Is that a line just to get me to come over? I mean, clearly all my stuff is here."

"You don't need your stuff yet. And yes, it's a line. Fall for it, I'm begging you." He paused to nip at her lips, drawing forth contented sighs from them both as they shared in the high that came whenever they kissed. "I want to make you dinner. And not for nothing, but I really can help you with this stuff. I work remotely as an assistant for Joss Motors. It's not as complicated as your gig, but I can help you better train your assistant, so you don't have to take your work on vacation."

"Remote assistant, eh?"

Cordray bobbed his head. "The world likes it best when I'm out of sight, so I have to make sure I understand my role and my boss' goals. I can help you with this." As if they were magnetized, Cordray's lips found their way to hers once again. "Let me help you, Story."

The desire to keep her tightly-wound system away from scrutinizing eyes she hoped to impress weighed heavy on her, making her want to shoo him out the door so he didn't see the mess for what it was. She'd tried to form a plan for her permanent leave of absence, but each time a project threatened to leave her hands, she clung tighter, not wanting to relinquish what little control she had over the remainder of her life.

Then Cordray kissed her again and again, and she realized how very much she wanted to be near him, even if it meant exposing her vulnerability, and the imperfections in her system. "You want to cook for me?"

"Only you," he sighed, and then his eyes widened, as if only just catching himself exposing too much of his hand too soon. "Let's go. Leave all this here."

Rory wanted to argue, but didn't let go of his hand. Instead, she stayed by his side as they walked along a trail that connected the scattered private homes.

Cordray's cabin was militaristically tidy, with no patience for knickknacks or useless decorations. It possessed a similar layout to Henry's cabin, with a spacious living room, a dining room off to the side, and a kitchen with an island in the center. The tall windows were different, though, as Henry had a wall in the back with a few normal-sized windows that could be easily blocked out. Cordray's kitchen welcomed the light, giving the woods an open invitation to cook with him as he busied about, waving his hand at a pan and cutting board, and catching them as they floated toward him in the air. "There's a pen and paper in the drawer there. Pull it out and have a seat."

Rory tugged the stool away from the island and climbed atop it, wishing she felt tall and capable. "Okay, I'm ready."

Cordray started chopping up an onion while the pan heated a drizzle of oil. "I want you to make a list of everything you're in charge of. A detailed list with all your tasks, down to returning emails. Don't leave anything out."

Rory's eyes widened. "I'm not sure this paper's big enough." Still, she complied, her anxiety rising as she began writing out the many items that she'd taken upon herself. Though she knew running the Foundation required a lot of work, she didn't realize how much she was doing until she ran out of room on the paper and had to turn it over to continue on the back. Item after item weighted her shoulders, pinching her eyebrows together in consternation as she scolded herself for stepping away from the organization for this long.

Cordray dumped the onions in the pan, bringing a lively sizzle into the kitchen. He left Rory to her list while he chopped up bell peppers and mushrooms, and then added those to the pan after the onions started browning. A zucchini was quickly julienned and tossed into the mix.

Rory's eyes left her paper only when she watched him flip the pan's contents with a flick of his wrist. The onions and mushrooms were fragrant, and her stomach screamed at her for skipping lunch. She'd gone too long without kissing him, but she tried to remind herself that she was an adult and should finish a task before devolving into a lust-addled teenager.

When Cordray threw in a handful of beansprouts, Rory realized she'd been captivated by his movements at the expense of finishing off her list. She went back to her task, feeling the weight of all that she'd run away from crowding out the space in her brain she'd reclaimed during their nature walk.

"Finished," she said, and slid the paper and pen away from her. The granite countertop had flecks of light blue and silver in the black, which she traced with her fingernail to keep her eyes from darting back to the paper that overwhelmed her.

"I was just about to say the same thing." He drizzled a healthy dose of soy sauce into the pan, and then shaved in a teaspoon of fresh ginger, finishing the whole thing off with a pinch of sea salt. "Let me see your list." His eyes poured over the many lines, his eyebrows pulling together as he frowned. "You realize this is a problem, right? Because if you don't see how wrong this is, then we've got a bigger issue on our hands."

"Is this you helping? You promised help and food. I'm this close to taking that entire pan and leaving you with my list."

He chuckled at her sass and set the paper back down in front of her. "Today I want you to pick four things and hand them off. Four things only, and off your plate completely. So far off your radar, that you won't have to think about them after today. Take a few minutes and call your assistant. Train her, explain it all, and then let it go."

Rory frowned at him. "It's not that simple."

"Nothing about giving up control is simple, but this isn't an option anymore." He tapped the page. "You're hiding in your work. That's not why you created this Foundation."

Rory pursed her lips, wondering when it was that they'd crossed over into the realm of him being able to give such constructive insight into her life. "Four things?"

"And you can pick which ones. But it has to be four, and it has to be now." He served up the food and set her plate in front of her on the island. He trotted into his bedroom and brought out a worn paperback, taking up residence in the stool next to hers. The food was hot, so he flipped open his book to somewhere in the middle and read quietly while Rory chose four things from her list, and then explained to her assistant over the phone how to handle said tasks without intervention from her.

By the time Rory ended the call, her food had cooled from piping hot, finally ready to be consumed. "I can't believe I just did that."

Cordray closed his thriller and placed his palm on her back, rubbing in soothing circles. "And would you look at that? The world didn't end."

Rory's mouth drew to the side. "Well, we'll see. This smells amazing, by the way."

They exchanged lighthearted stories while they ate. The conversation traded off naturally, as if they'd been comfortable with each other forever. To celebrate her workload lightening, they made out on his couch for an hour, thrilling in the freedom of being alone together.

The next few days were much the same, with a couple alterations as they fell into a rhythm. Not long after the sun rose, Cordray came over and they ate breakfast together while he worked on his laptop. Each morning, she took four more things off her list, training her assistant remotely until she felt confident she wouldn't have to reclaim the tasks as her own.

Then the two would go for a nature walk, holding hands and swapping kisses that took on varying shades of sweet and sultry. They packed picnic lunches and ate next to the brook atop the felled tree. They had quickly claimed it as their special spot, and spent many hours straddling the trunk while confessing the highs and lows of their differing paths that had led them to adulthood. Cordray pointed out the different wildlife, and the unique tracks they made in the dirt while Rory let her senses be enamored with the many flowers that seemed to bloom just for them.

Dinner was always shared at Cordray's home, and they ended each evening after a frenzied hour of making out like teenagers on his couch.

When Cordray walked her home well after dark, she turned on the front porch and draped her arms around his shoulders, leaning into him as they kissed again and again. He was on the step below her, which put her on equal footing with him.

It wasn't until he dipped his chin downward to break the kiss, his forehead pressed to hers, that she noticed the sadness marring his features in the moonlight. "How long do I have with you?"

"As long as you'd like," she replied languidly. It was intoxicating to be so near him, to kiss him whenever she pleased. She stroked the nape of his neck, loving that she could be the one to satiate his craving for touch.

"How long until you have to go back to your life? How long do we get to keep each other like this?"

Rory's libido crested and then crashed, leaving her feeling a slight chill in the air. "I'm not sure what day it is."

"Maybe that's a sign that we shouldn't let this fade away. Maybe we should try for something more than a week in the woods."

Rory's heart swelled beyond what she'd allowed herself to hope for. There hadn't been much room or reason for optimism in her life, but now here it was, standing in front of her, asking her questions she'd never permitted herself to consider. "I like the sound of that. What would that look like?"

Cordray let out a gust of pent-up nerves, drawing her in tighter so their stomachs were flush as he kissed her over and over again. Leaves and errant sticks floated in the air behind him, as if they wanted a peek at their master's happiness. It seemed the magic followed him around like a puppy, eager to please. "I have no idea. I only care that we're both willing to give it a real, honest try. This doesn't happen for me, Story. I know better than to let a good thing slip through my fingers."

"This has been the best week of my life," she admitted, toying with the cropped hair at the base of his neck. Again, he shivered, making her feel powerful in her femininity.

"Then let's sleep on it. Tomorrow we'll figure out how to hold onto each other."

His gloved hands were always respectful, but Rory could tell they were both wanting more than a handful of chaste kisses. "Tomorrow," she promised him, running her fingers over the hard planes of his chest before she bid him goodnight. They were a good match – she was unable to stop touching him, and every time her hands made contact with any part of his body, it seemed to heal a deep-seeded wound he'd harbored for too many years.

Rory moved into the cabin, utter rapture making her feel as if she was floating. It wasn't until the sound of a man's voice broke the solace of the silence that Rory yelped, flicking on the lights to reveal the intruder.

The slow teasing tone made her shrink with chagrin. "Well, well, well, who on earth was that?"

8

CORDRAY'S OFFER

*T*he sun was just barely up, but Rory hadn't been able to sleep much, instead opting to work at the kitchen table until Remus awoke and then joined her for coffee and paperwork. "I was doing just fine out here. Remind me again why you assumed I needed a chaperone?"

"It was either me, Benjamin, or the entire military force. You're welcome."

"I guess you are the lesser evil of all those options."

"And I'm actually taking a few things off your plate. You were truly going to do all this by yourself during your grand escape?"

Rory dropped her pen on the table and folded her arms over her chest. "How'd you even find me? Did Henry squeal?"

"No. I found you because I'm amazing. Though, Henry

is a terrible liar. I knew he knew where you were, so I started visiting his long list of properties." Remus picked up a contract and showed it to her. "This one's missing your signature."

"I was getting to it."

"You're still not going to tell me about the mysterious man on the porch from last night?"

"How about we talk about your love life first. How long do you imagine that conversation might be?"

Remus grimaced. "Pass. You were supposed to be home yesterday, you realize. You asked for one week. That you think Benjamin has the patience or the willpower to stay away from his charge for a moment longer than the allotted time shows how little you understand his loyalty to our family. He's been downright surly."

Guilt tugged at Rory's features. "I didn't want him to worry, but I knew there was no way he'd let me have a week to myself."

"You're right on that point. Expect the longest lecture of your life when you get back. He treated me to a warmup of it yesterday."

"Sorry about that."

"You've got your annual exam tomorrow. Did you forget?"

Her spine stiffened and her mouth stayed in a straight line of displeasure. "I'm a Deadpulse, Uncle Remus. I'll still be one after the test. I don't see why I have to take it again."

"Now, now, let the Baron have his fun. It tricks him into thinking he has some semblance of power in the world. Like giving a baby a pacifier instead of the real thing."

Breathing out through her nose, Rory did her best to steady herself. "This will be my last test, and after that, the Baron will have exactly what he wants – for me to be the reason Dad's legacy isn't passed down."

Remus reached across the table and touched her hand. "You being able to perform magic isn't a requirement for running the council."

Rory met her uncle's gaze with dubiousness tainting her optimism. "I'll let you go on believing that if you need to."

Remus closed his eyes and hung his head. "One problem at a time. I need to see the Feldman contract. They've been hemming and hawing over details that shouldn't matter."

Rory jumped when a knock sounded at the front door. She made to answer it, but Remus was out of his chair, motioning for her to stay back.

Rory bumped him, trying to push him backwards. "It's nothing to worry about. Cordray always comes over for breakfast."

Raising his eyebrow, he took in her piqued tone and the excitement that came over her at a hint of Cordray's presence. "He does, does he? Very well, let's meet this fine young man."

She rolled her eyes at him. "You sound like Dad."

"Yes, and he's about to meet a member of your family for the first time." Remus' posture was stiff as he opened the door a few inches. "May I help you?"

Cordray looked taken aback at the man filling the doorway. "Oh, I'm sorry. I was looking for Rory. Is she around?"

Remus tapped his chin, glancing upward. "Rory? I don't know of any Rory."

Shoving her uncle aside, she shot him a scolding look as he devolved into airy giggles. "Ignore him. He's enjoying this way too much. Come on in. Or actually, let's go out. That would be far less complicated."

Cordray postured, his chin lifting at the challenge. "I'm not afraid of complicated." Then he extended his hand to the man he recognized from the papers. "Cordray Phillips, sir. I just started seeing your niece, and I'd like to see a lot more of her." When the tawdry implications of his words dawned on him, panic struck his features, widening his eyes. "I mean I'd like to see her more often."

Remus permitted an amused smile to play on his lips as he shook Cordray's gloved hand. "Then you know who I am?"

"Everyone knows who you are. You're Remus Johnstone, the student who countered Malaura's curse when Rory was born."

Remus stood a little straighter in his gray slacks, lavender dress shirt and loosened tie. "That's correct. Then you must know how very closely I watch my niece. Her happiness is second only to her safety in my book." His eyes tracked the leaves and twigs that levitated behind Cordray, suspended in air without obvious effort. A zip of fascination lit Remus' features as he studied the display of Cordray's magic.

"Yes, sir." Cord's mouth stiffened, and he brushed his hand over his shoulder in a jerky motion, as if commanding nature to knock it off already.

There was an uncomfortable pause, but then Remus' face broke out into a wide grin. "Come on in. Tell me all about yourself."

"No," Rory ruled, her face stern as she warned her uncle with her icy gaze that he shouldn't interfere.

"No?" Remus feigned shock, touching his chest with a scoff of disbelief. "I only want to meet the man who's occupying your days. I'm hurt you wouldn't want to introduce me."

"You're going to interrogate him, and we only just met a week ago. Let it be fun before it's dowsed in duty and all of our family's seriousness."

Cordray stood straighter, his chest puffing. "Thank you, sir. I think I'll join you," he said, moving into the cabin with a look that told Remus he wasn't going away. Then quietly to Rory, he added, "I told you last night that I wanted us to find a way to be together. I still don't know how to make that happen, but I do know it's never going to happen if you think I can't handle your uncle ruffling my feathers a little."

Remus nodded at Cordray appreciatively and, noting the lack of squirreliness in the man, decided on the spot that any further teasing or strong-arming wasn't necessary. In standing up to her family's scrutiny, it was clear Cordray was settled enough with Rory that he wouldn't be scared off easily when the press descended on the couple. Remus poured Cordray a mug of coffee and cleared off a space at the table, motioning for him to sit.

Cordray waited until Rory took her place at the table, and then took the spot next to her, uniting himself with her to make it clear to everyone at the table that he was in this for Rory, and wouldn't be dissuaded.

The small exchanges of chitchat pushed Rory to reach for her napkin, so she could rest it on her lap and tear at the edges surreptitiously. Remus and Cordray talked about the weather, work, and about living in the country versus the city.

"This is quite the hike from Rory's home near the capital. Are you planning on keeping in touch after today?"

Rory narrowed her eyes at her uncle. "This feels like a conversation that is none of your business."

Cordray reached over and laced his gloved fingers through hers, calming both their nerves. "Actually, I made a few calls last night. A friend of mine has a condo he's not using that he'd be willing to rent out to me for a while. But I won't move there unless it's what Rory wants."

Rory's sharp intake of breath erased Remus from her

mind altogether. She took in the composed look on Cordray's face with wonder. "Are you serious?"

"About you? I thought I made it clear that I was very serious about us. I said I'd find a way to make this work, so this is my attempt. If it's too much or too fast, I won't do it. Entirely up to you."

Rory balked at him, turning in her chair, her knees bumping against his. "But you don't like living near people."

"I could make my peace with it if it meant I got to see you on the regular."

Rory studied his face for signs of flight that might make for a grudging disposition if he was pushing himself into something he wasn't ready for. But there wasn't a trace of worry on his face, only a slight tightening of his gaze at her possible rejection. "Remus, could you give us a minute? Let's go for a walk, Cord."

"Whatever you want, Story." Cordray stood and offered his hand to her, ignoring Remus' giddy grin as the two walked out together.

The moment nature was their only witness, Rory whirled on him. "Tell me the absolute truth, are you going to resent me for making you move to the city? Because as much as I want to be with you, it's not an option for me to pick up and move out here. I couldn't reciprocate."

Cordray pulled her to stand in his embrace, his arms loosely coiling around her as if they'd been waiting for the chance to hold something they deemed precious. "First off, you're not making me do anything. This was my suggestion because I know civilian life isn't an option for you. But I understand that this is moving fast, so you have to be sure you want this, and then I'll come out to the city to give us a shot."

Rory buried her face in his chest, reveling in the solid feel of him. "You'll keep your cabin here, though, in case my life is too difficult for you?"

"It won't be, but yes, I'm keeping my cabin. Then if you want to escape, you won't have to break a window to this place."

"I work," she hedged. "I'm at the office a lot."

"You don't say." He drew her chin up so he could look into her eyes. "I work, too. And I get that you've got your own life. I just want to be part of whatever makes you smile."

Relief flooded Rory's features, curving the corners of her mouth upward before she lifted herself onto her toes. The kiss was sweet at first – a promise of better things to come. The languid pace of their pledge awakened parts of them that had been largely untapped through most of their lives. That seemed to be the way with them – every kiss presented a new awakening.

When Cordray's arms tightened around her hips, Rory couldn't help but draw her fingernails across the nape of his neck, coaxing out a guttural noise from him that drove her to deepen the kiss. Her lips parted slightly so she could sweep her tongue across his. Her body molded around his, bending and curving as his hand reached down to cup the back of her thigh.

His breath was choppy, giving Rory a heady sensation of power that she felt finally ready for. So much of her life had been doomed and decided before she'd uttered her first word. To be able to throw life a curveball and live with such satiated hunger bloomed parts of her soul she'd assumed it was fine to live without.

But now she knew better. She resolved herself that she wouldn't hold back anymore. She wouldn't resign herself to a mundane existence, but would chase after whatever it was that made her feel so very much alive.

She kissed Cordray over and over, not caring how many minutes ticked by. For the first time, she was free, so she clung to the one who'd done his best to give her so many moments of passion, and hopefully, what would be many more to come.

9

FAILING THE ANNUAL EXAM

"*N*o, Lord Bartholomew, I don't have a Pulse," Rory droned, frustrated that she had to go through the questionnaire yet again. Every year, it was the same old stodgy man with thin-rimmed glasses perched on the end of his bulbus nose, looking like they might dive off his face at the slightest hint of a sneeze.

Rory dipped into her pocket to run her fingers over the paperclip inside. It wasn't just any standard silver fastener, but a gray coated one. Cordray had found out her favorite color and purchased a box of paperclips in her preferred shade. She'd received a golden music box from King Hubert on her last birthday, but the gift of paperclips had soared into first place in her heart. Of course, they were too special to use on like, paper, so Rory had taken to carrying one or two in her pocket at all times, just to remind herself that someone thought she was special enough to buy paperclips for. It was particularly helpful when she found herself in the throes of failing an exam.

"No Pulse still," the proctor noted, his wrinkled, fat fingers tensing as he scribbled in his notebook. "Not the slightest inkling of being able to shoot an impulse into another person?"

"No, sir." *Next time, why don't you just ask me if I'm useless?*

"Very well, Miss Aurora. Let's see what you can do this year."

Rory pulled in a deep breath and let it slide through her parted lips in hopes it would center her, as Remus instructed. She'd seen countless others do this, and had gone through all the classes, but still, it did nothing to increase her magic output.

"You're to levitate the teacup, dear."

She loathed the sweetheart names the elders gave her. Everyone else on the council was called by their first name, title or surname, and was respected as an adult. She was spoken to as if she was still five years old, with an unfettered passion for wearing pigtails. Though, she had actually known the proctor since she'd been a little girl, so she tried not to be too annoyed with Lord Bartholomew's old habits.

Closing her eyes, she reached out her hands, wishing she would give herself a spontaneous aneurism or something to escape this annual reminder of her shortcomings. It was a full five minutes the proctor gave her. Because of who her father was, he'd even consented to conduct the test in her own home, to preserve her pride and the family's reputation. Though, truly, everyone knew that she was the dud in the powerful family. There had even been gossip that not a single ounce of magic could be found in her blood. When Rory had read that gem years ago, she'd doubled her efforts at her Foundation, vowing that she would not be a joke to her people.

Rory tried to push out the reminders of failure and rumors of doom, and refocused on the teacup, pleading with it to please, please, please just move already. "I'd like one more minute," she requested with fire in her eyes when the proctor clicked his stopwatch and called time.

"Take as long as you need, dear. I've got to pack up my notes, anyway. You gave it a good try." Then he got out his phone and punched in three digits.

The voice on the other end was loud, to compensate for Lord Bartholomew's aged hearing. "Did she fail again?"

"Yes. You can send in the replacement."

Her mother and father weren't allowed in the room during the testing, only her tutor. Remus was firm with the proctor from his place in the chair, his fingers tented in front of his chest. "If the Chancellor's daughter said she needs another minute, that's exactly what you'll give her."

Lord Bartholomew pushed his glasses up again, and shot Remus a withering look that made the saggy skin of his eyelids droop even further. "She can take all the minutes she likes, but that teacup's not moving."

"Your disrespect will be noted," Remus replied with a measured scolding to his tone. "Go on, Rory. Just like we practiced."

The minute came and went, and the teacup sat on the ornate end table – a giant middle finger in the face of Rory's best efforts. She reached in her pocket and fingered the gray paperclip again, wishing her life could be a little less grim.

When the tall brass doors at the back of the maroon-painted ballroom opened, the Baron strode in with a man Rory had never seen before on his heels. Being an alpha male was a given for many in the kingdom, but some of them took it to the extreme. The slicked black hair, brooding eyes, and jaw that was set to never crack a smile greeted her with a tight nod. The Baron was in his sixties, but his lack of congeniality made him seem about a hundred to Rory. "Miss Johnstone."

The proctor called Rory's parents in, and they ran into the ballroom with hopeful looks on their faces. "Did she pass? How did it go? Rory, no matter what, we love you, and we're so proud of you," they said all at once as they hugged their only daughter. They bore matching black hair, fair complexions and unmitigated kindness in their eyes.

Benjamin came in behind them, posting himself at the exit in his usual bodyguard demeanor. Ever since her escape into the woods, he'd scarcely let her out of his sight.

The Baron looked down his nose at the indulgent exchange. "See, this is the problem. She did literally nothing, and she's praised. Well, all that stops today. Remus, you've failed as her tutor. You're officially dismissed."

Remus' eyes hardened, but he didn't give the Baron the stunned reaction the man was hoping for. "If only you could dismiss me. I'm not on your payroll, Baron. Four citizens have gone missing this month, and yet you're concerning yourself with Rory. Don't you think that's perhaps... unusual for a grown man to think about a young woman so habitually?"

Rory pursed her lips through her shudder at her uncle's implications. She knew Remus made them only to needle at the Baron, who had a wandering eye for inappropriately younger women. She thanked her lucky stars for his utter hatred of her because her title would always be higher than his.

The Baron raised his wet nose in the air. "Those four citizens are Lethals. It's hardly the scandal you're making it out to be. You know how Lethals are. They get fed up with a silver spoon not being handed to them, and they take off for obscurity. That, or they're running from a crime they've committed."

"Tell me again about this enlightened view of the world you have," Remus said as he rolled his eyes.

The Baron's tone turned harsh at the mild scolding. "Stop deflecting. You've failed, so you're to step down as Aurora's tutor. You're being replaced by Tyren. He's the best. Trained my son perfectly. Calvin graduated top of his class, and heads up the Society for the Future Elite." The Baron's bony hand motioned to the bull-like brick wall, who appeared to have zero personality. "Tyren is more than a capable tutor, and forgive me, but he uses his magic for practical things. He was working under the king's advisor earlier this year. Tyren will be her new tutor, and he'll get her all caught up to speed. Our Chancellor will have a family deserving of the hype, finally. If not, I see no reason why his rule should be passed down to Aurora, simply over the mere convenience of bloodline. Frankly, a Chancellor who can't see how flawed the system is shouldn't hold the highest chair on the council anyway."

Remus and Rory both looked as if someone had slapped them. Rory's parents took offense at the slam on their family with their noses in the air and snarls on their lips. Mrs. Johnstone stepped back, but Mr. Johnstone took a bold step forward. "You dare insult me in my own home? Performing magic is but a portion of what we do for the world. If you want to vie for my position in the council, go after me, not my daughter. It shouldn't matter whether or not she can cast charms. It matters that she can look at all the issues objectively, and is dedicated to serving the people."

"Ah, but you see, that's where you're wrong. If she cannot wield magic, then how can she be expected to make decisions that affect its uses? Do you see how much more of a problem it will be if we have a woman without a

Pulse voting on magical issues? The proposal to install trackers in the Lupine was shot down by a margin of one measly vote."

Rory stood firm in her decision she'd made an impassioned speech about during the last council meeting. "The Lupine used to be humans, Baron. They should have every right to walk about freely, as we do. Would you like me deciding to put a tracker under your skin?"

The Baron's nostrils flared. "Dear girl, you are insufferable."

Rory raised her chin, determined not to disgrace her family. "Then I'll forfeit my vote on all magical issues until I can perform charms, if that's what it comes down to – if this is how petty you're going to be. But you'll leave my family out of this. My father is the best Chancellor Avondale's ever seen. Unemployment is down, minimum wage is up, and even insufferable elitists like yourself have freedom of speech enough to run down whomever you wish. Tell me, Baron, do you enjoy the illusion of power? Does it make you feel like a big man to subtly threaten our family's rule?"

Benjamin stiffened from his spot near the exit, but didn't interfere, his arms tucked behind his back. His job was to assuage physical attacks on the Chancellor's daughter, not the verbal ones that cut her just as deep. He watched for any move that might be too close, just so he had the opportunity to pounce on the Baron, who'd long proved to be an annoyance to his employer.

Stefan postured beside his daughter. "It's enough. If you wish to take my spot on the council, you'll have to work far harder than running down my daughter over a blip in her long list of accomplishments. King Hubert decides if she is fit for her future post. If you cannot respect your king, then perhaps that's something you should take up with him."

The Baron looked down his nose at Rory, and then glared at the Chancellor. "How your imagination does run away with you, Stefan. If Rory's willing to forfeit her vote on all magical issues, I'll take that as a win for the community as a whole."

"You'll do no such thing, Rory," her mother said with a protective arm around her daughter. Leah Johnstone had the same fire in her eyes, and grace enough to communicate it without shouting. "The council is shortsighted if they think non-magical people have no value to add. If anything, we should appreciate that there's diversity on the council. The people as a whole take non-magical folk for granted. You act as if Rory can't tie her own shoes."

"And you act as if all it takes to rule is tying one's shoes."

Mrs. Johnstone let out a shrill noise of indignation. The temper in her eyes that she'd passed down to her daughter flared dangerously. "You'll watch your words, Baron. My daughter founded and runs the largest organization that keeps our schools running and provides education to all of Avondale. If not for her, that burden would be on the government, whose budget cannot possibly stretch that far. My daughter has proved herself to be a fiscal asset to the council. You'll not be dismissive of her contributions just because she ties her shoes differently than you."

The Baron had thin skin stretched taught across too many sharply-angled bones. "One of the tasks of the council is to regulate dangerous Pulsing. Your daughter has no value to us, and thus, neither does her vote."

Remus moved to Leah's other side, hemming Rory in with his protection, and shielding his family as best he could. The vein in the Chancellor's forehead was beginning to throb noticeably, which meant that Remus needed to intervene before his older brother debased himself with a fruitless argument. "'Us' isn't decided by you. That's why there's a council."

As if expecting this, the Baron reached into his cloak and pulled out a piece of parchment that had thirteen signatures on it scribbled under the demand for the Chancellor's resignation. "That's a majority decision. If your daughter doesn't perform to our standards, your bloodline has finally run dry, and is of little use to us. You'll still serve on the council, of course, but not as its leader."

The Chancellor snatched the parchment without looking at it, his eyes fixed only on the Baron. "There is no vote that can officially take place without me as the head presiding. This piece of rubbish means nothing to me, my family, or the community at large. Yet another reason you will never sit in my seat. You pay no attention to the law, only your own agenda. How many names on this list did you buy?" Then, an inch from the Baron's long nose, the Chancellor tore the parchment in two.

Remus floated the document in the air, displaying the slow ripping as the pieces of all the Baron's cajoling and strong-arming were littered onto the floor like confetti, celebrating the Baron's job poorly done.

Though the Baron was livid at the technicality being called out, he maintained his prideful posture. "Be that as it may, Lord Bartholomew is head of the Board of Education. After careful consideration, he's ruled that if Aurora failed her exam this time around, she would be reassigned to a new tutor." He snapped his fingers at Tyren, and then turned his nose up at Rory. "You may have been too good to accept my son's offer for marriage, but you'll not say no to a proper tutor."

Rory stiffened. She'd detested Calvin since they'd been children, when he'd been too superior to get his hands dirty by playing in the mud with her. As he'd grown handsome enough to get away with being a prat, the other girls in their classes had fallen for his charms, but Rory wanted nothing to do with his hands that had no problem getting dirty now. His own ego led him to ask her out because of who her father was. Her family's position of power and prestige was second only to the king's. When she'd given Calvin a flat, unwavering no, his spoiled child syndrome came out, wanting what he couldn't have simply because it was denied him.

How she wanted to go public with her relationship with Cordray. They'd both never been happier. Still, for the sake of taking things slow so as not to scare him away with the throngs of people who would want interviews and to know every detail of his private life, they'd kept their relationship secret, spending most of their time together helping him move into his condo.

Rory rolled her shoulders back, reclaiming some of the dignity that always felt stripped bare after her annual exams. "Calvin asking for my hand was far more horrifying for me than it was for you, Baron. You might be ashamed to have me as part of your family if I ever lost my mind and accepted, but trust me, your son's childishness is far more an embarrassment to my family's standards."

The Chancellor was livid with the Baron, who was always trying to play the long con. "I'll decide who my daughter is alone with, and I haven't given my approval that her tutor should change. As her parent, I have that right."

Rory stiffened, not liking being spoken of as if she was five, and unable to make decisions about with whom she wanted to be alone. She didn't argue though, since she didn't want to be within ten feet of Tyren, who looked ready to bark out orders at the slightest infraction. She shoved her hand in her pocket, running her fingers over the gray paperclip, hoping for its presence to steady her nerves.

10

A FAILED TUTOR

"No, of course my job isn't interfering with my studies," Rory assured Tyren. "I've been studying. I know the material backwards and forwards; I just can't actually perform any of the charms."

Remus folded his arms over his chest, leaning against the wall in the Chancellor's mansion. He refused to sit, but also refused to leave his niece alone with anyone associated with the Baron.

Benjamin stood at the door, studying the new tutor with veiled disdain. Tyren was aggressive and condescending, but Benjamin said nothing, only inching forward if Tyren came close to touching his charge.

Tyren was in his forties, his bald head showing off the veins in his scalp that throbbed when he was frustrated. "You're not pushing yourself. If you know the text, you should be able to perform the spells."

Tyren never sat, but towered over Rory's chair in the parlor. The light mint-colored furniture was dainty, constructed of dark wood with vines and leaves carved into the legs. The subtle nod to nature was echoed onto the paintings of Avondale's tallest mountains that hung in gold frames on the walls. The décor was courtesy of Rory's mother, and Adam's mother, as well, before she'd passed. The two women had an eye for detail, designing several rooms to suit her daughter's pale complexion. Rory tried not to think about the tragedy that befell Adam's parents over a decade ago, but made a mental note to call Adam that evening to check up on him.

Rory sat like a china doll, her back rigid and her hands folded in her lap. "You've seen me try the charms. I've recited everything to you verbatim. Why don't you tell me what I'm doing wrong? I mean, the Baron insinuated that Uncle Remus failed as a tutor because I couldn't pass my exams." Rory kept her voice light, as she'd seen her mother do at tea parties when the gossip would get out of hand. "Perhaps you're a terrible tutor. I mean, me failing means that you're failing, correct?"

Remus smirked at his niece, sniggering at the politeness that was laced into her gall. "Tyren is far more educated than most, Rory. If he can't help you, then perhaps he should go back to school."

"Yes, I think I'll suggest some tutors for you to the Baron myself, Tyren. For your own good," she simpered.

Tyren's ears were red, as they often were when he was

trying to hold onto his temper during their lessons. The crimson wave swept across his bald head as he chewed on the more acerbic words he would never be allowed to spew at the Chancellor's daughter. "Recite the incantations again."

Rory didn't break eye contact with Tyren as she repeated not just the charm for object levitation, but the entire page of instructions that followed in the text. She'd read the book of spells enough times to know that it wasn't academic smarts she was lacking. There were some things you couldn't teach. She didn't have the raw talent needed to pull off such things, and after three weeks of being grilled every night by Tyren after work, she was tired of beating around the bush. It was seriously cutting into her time with Cordray, who was waiting in the dining room, talking shop with her father, as he always did on evenings where her schedule was not her own.

Once she recited the entire page of text for object levitation, she then moved onto the Latin translation that followed. The dead language so many had struggled with rolled off her tongue like honey. She didn't look away, nor did she allow him to interject.

It was when she moved onto the next spell that Tyren finally held up his hand. "Alright, alright. I get it."

Rory had worked late and rushed through dinner, all so she could get to these frustrating lessons. At least when Remus tutored her, they accomplished something. He would go over the origins of where the spell came from –

who cast it quite by accident, and what great battles led to the discovery of a whole new spell. Remus had always been fascinated with the unearthing of new magic, and how the world changed because of its ripple effect. Rory had more knowledge than most accomplished magicians about such things, but she'd never succeeded in putting them into practice.

After proving her knowledge, Rory finally held the control in the room, standing with her chin raised. "Apologize to Remus for the not-so-subtle digs on his abilities. My shortcomings are not his fault – nor are they yours. This is who I am. I've accepted it, and so will the council."

Tyren looked over to Remus with disdain. "The council will never accept a Deadpulse. You'll lose your right to vote, mark my words."

"If I do, then it'll be widely known that you've lost your touch. You failed, Tyren." She rolled her shoulders back, feeling liberated that she had the power to damn anyone with the verdict she'd had to face over and over again. "You let your people down by not getting me to be able to cast a simple spell. I mean, come on. Children can levitate these small, immobile objects." She sounded confident and calculating, but she was simply vomiting all the things told to her over the years that she'd had to stomach.

Tyren slammed his book shut. "I'll not put up with your mouth. We'll try this again tomorrow, but without your attitude."

"What attitude? I'm merely repeating the things your

precious Baron has said to my face. Are you so sensitive that you can't take criticism from your employer?" She turned her chin toward her uncle. "Remus, what is it your boss says to you?"

Remus smirked at her. "You usually tell me that you love me."

"I do. You're the vice president of the Johnstone Foundation because I trust you to be brilliant and capable." She leaned forward, breaking her perfect posture to drive her point home. "Don't worry, Tyren. You'll get there one day. Until then, I'm sure working for the Baron is bliss on ice. I'm so, so happy for you, living your dream by tutoring a Deadpulse. It seems like a fitting use of your extensive, and no doubt expensive education." She sighed when Tyren's cheeks flamed an even deeper shade of red after Benjamin broke his stoic demeanor with a chuckle. "Oh, I hate to think what might happen if you failed. The Baron doesn't do well with failures."

Tyren's thick fingers were shaking as he moved forward to tower over her, every muscle poised to pounce.

11

MARRYING CALVIN

Rory didn't react when Tyren puffed out his chest and leaned forward to press his knuckles atop the back of her chair, because she knew Benjamin would be on top of it. Though Tyren hadn't touched her, Benjamin cleared the gap between the two and shoved the muscular man backward. "Too close," he warned without apology. "You'll not forget your place. She's the Chancellor's daughter, and you're her tutor."

Remus shoved Tyren's books against his chest and held the door open to get rid of eighty percent of the tension in the room. When the door shut, he exhaled. "I nearly high-fived you when you threw in that bit about the Baron."

Rory smiled, but went back to her rigid posture. "Anyone implying you're not the best there is out there is what sets me off in a blind rage."

Calvin stalked in, his walk its usual stilted, jerky gait,

as if he moved with something perpetually lodged between his butt cheeks. His long nose and sharply angular features matched his father's almost exactly. "I see you've managed to set Tyren off. That's quite a gift. He's usually unshakeable."

"I thought you'd gone home," Rory said by way of a greeting. She took in his haughty eyes and coifed black hair with a grimace. He'd started using even more product than the usual stickiness that kept his hair immoveable. He was only an inch taller than her, but she felt like he was far, far shorter when he was frustrated.

"I was waiting until your lessons were over to take you out."

Rory stood and stacked her books, which Benjamin took from her. "I'm afraid I'm unavailable. Thank you for the offer, though."

Calvin scoffed and glanced at Benjamin, who had twenty years on them both. "You're not allowed to marry below your station. Bodyguards are far below us."

Benjamin's jaw tightened, but Remus laughed. "Oh, wow. Benjamin's older than I am. You know how particular the Chancellor is concerning who comes sniffing around his only daughter. Do you really think Benjamin would still be standing if he was trying to make a move on Rory? He held her when she was born."

Calvin tried to smooth over his misstep, recalling his highbrow manners. "Forgive me, but I couldn't imagine any man being with you day in and day out and not falling head over heels for you, Roar. Your beauty is enough to make even those below our station entertain foolish ideas."

She detested the nickname Calvin had given her when they'd been kids. It had been a joke – that she'd been too quiet, so the name was akin to dubbing a large man "Tiny". "Everyone's beneath you, Calvin. I'm not sure why you're here. Clearly I'm not as accomplished as you. Why don't you ask out Serena? She's a far better match. I'm sure the Baron would prefer her on your arm rather than me."

"You're dismissed," Calvin barked to Benjamin and Remus, neither of whom moved an inch. He huffed in exasperation when he realized his word wasn't enough here. At his home, the servants scattered when they saw him coming. Here, he was somewhat of a joke, which made him more irritable than usual. "Walk with me."

"How about I walk you to the door on your way out?" Rory offered with a lightness in her tone that suggested all memory of him would cease the moment he exited the mansion.

Calvin extended his elbow, as was customary when courting, but Rory didn't take the bait. She kept a healthy three feet of space between them as they walked down the cobblestone hallway. The palace and Adam's castle had mostly wood or marble flooring, and were decked with the most expensive rugs. Rory's mother preferred the whimsy of shaved cobblestone on the main floor, and hardwood on the above floors.

Calvin kept his chin raised while he spoke. "You haven't been to the new gallery downtown, have you?"

"I'm afraid I haven't made the time. Is it nice?"

"More than nice. It's exquisite. I'll take you there this weekend. Saturday morning at ten?"

"I work late Friday nights, and have to study on Saturdays to prepare for the amazing new tutor your father arranged for me. Thank you, but no." She knew no waffling would fly with Calvin. If he saw the tiniest hint of interest, he would never let up.

Calvin's superior chortle made Rory's skin crawl. "Work? You're too funny. You know you don't need a job, right? We have several fortunes between the two of us."

"I love my job. Not everything in life is about money." Rory shot him a controlled look, but a little of her exasperation shone through. "Calvin, you don't like spending time with me. We have nothing in common. We don't share the same ideals. Nothing that I am is anything you respect, other than my title. There's no reason for you to keep coming by."

His shoulders hunched inward conspiratorially as they walked. He lowered his voice to keep his true wishes away from Remus and Benjamin. "Just think of it. The Baron's son and the Chancellor's daughter? We could do absolutely anything. The world won't have seen a more powerful union before us. Even if Prince Henry takes a wife someday, there's no eligible woman who has as much political weight to throw around as you do. Our mansion would be bigger, our votes would be weightier. All of it, more." A note of deviousness sneaked into his words. "We could be more powerful than even our fathers."

Rory bristled, but tried to keep her sneer tucked away. "My father is the best thing that's ever happened to the council. It's fine that you don't like your father; that's to be expected. No one likes the Baron. But my household isn't yours. I'm content being who I am, and my family likes that about me."

"But who you are is so much more than running a charity. Your time is running out, Roar. You'll be twenty-five in three months."

She stopped walking, counting to three before speaking, to make sure she didn't lose her temper. Her hand went into her pocket, her finger stroking the gray paperclip, which served to center her. "When I decide to marry, it won't be with someone who assumes my passions are decidedly less." She paused at the door and undid the latch. "I am not less, Calvin. And I'm also not so desperate as to settle for someone who assumes I am."

Calvin stopped before crossing over the threshold, taking his black fur coat from the rack. "Know this: I am your only hope of staying on the council. Your father's time in the sun is coming to an end. Soon his words won't hold the weight they do now. Then where will you be? I could provide for you. I could guarantee you always have a vote, Deadpulse though you are. Look around! There is no other man lining up to court you. I'm literally your last chance at happiness."

Remus knew Rory could handle herself, but he'd endured enough of Calvin's needling. He shoved Calvin out the door, posturing as the bully faltered on the stoop. "She just said she was happy, and that's got nothing to do with you."

Remus slammed the door shut on Calvin's indignant spluttering, leaning against it as he took in the heaviness that weighted his niece. Most people didn't understand why a young woman of her status and wealth chose to work at a place that was fast-paced and occasionally high-stress on top of all her other responsibilities, but her parents, Remus and the staff got it. She was an utter failure at all things magic, but she'd found her niche in the humanitarian world. Instead of squashing that potential, her parents nurtured it, letting her be who she was without apology.

"I'll make sure Calvin leaves," Benjamin offered. Before he exited, he paused next to his charge. "If you marry him, I'll quit, and then I'll turn all your clothes pink."

Rory chuckled, and then reached up to peck her guard's cheek. "Well, then it's settled. No matrimonial bliss for Calvin and me."

"Go be blissful with that Cordray guy. He appreciates you. Don't settle for that sniveling weasel." Benjamin had made his peace with Cordray, but still called him "that Cordray guy", just in case things went south.

"Thanks, Benjamin." She watched him leave, holding a handful of gratitude in her heart for his devotion to her family that never ran dry.

Remus didn't know how to comfort his niece after her grueling tutoring lessons, so he opted for shtick. "You look a little stressed. Maybe you should go to the movies with Calvin, get married and pop out a few kids. That sounds like a recipe for happiness if I ever heard one. I mean, with a condescending offer like that, who could say no?"

Rory let out a sarcastic snort. "Do me a favor? If I'm ever considering his offer, haul me off into the woods and shoot me."

"I'll even let you pick the gun. Come on. I know a certain someone who's been waiting for your lessons to end. Enchanting though your father is, I'm sure Cordray would much prefer your company."

Rory took him up on the offer of an escort, walking down the hallway with her uncle's protective arm tight around her shoulders.

FIRST DATE JITTERS

It was the first day Rory had gone into the office without feeling waves of stress. By taking four tasks off of her plate each day, hiring two more assistants to work alongside Francesca, and training her staff to handle the workload Rory had championed by herself for years, the death grip she'd had on her Foundation began to loosen. There were even whole three-minute periods where she found herself without anything to do.

It wasn't until Cordray called that she realized how calm the whole office felt. Everyone was handling their zones, and understood what work needed to be done, and by when. "Hey, you," she said, cradling her phone with her shoulder as she shut her office door. She was wary of saying his name in an area where anyone could hear it, or see the telling smile that caressed her face whenever she spoke to him. "How's your day going?"

"It's going well, actually. My boss closed a big account today because of research I did, and I wanted to celebrate. How would you feel about me taking you out to lunch? Can you step away for an hour?"

Rory froze, her voice lowering to a whisper. "Are you joking? People would see us."

She could hear the joy in his chuckle. "That's kind of the idea. We've been dating in secret for a month. I think it's time to take the training wheels off this thing."

Rory scarcely comprehended the rest of their conversation, only when and where she was going to meet him. She grabbed her purse before heading not to the entrance, but to Remus' office, knocking lightly on the door. When he let her in, she shut the door after slipping inside, her eyes wide. "I have a favor to ask."

"If you want me to buy you a unicorn, my money's a little tied up in a new business deal your father talked me into. And by 'talked me into', I mean I was more than a little tipsy, the sneak. He knows my weakness for good whiskey. Next week."

Rory rolled her eyes at his joke. "Cord asked me to go to lunch with him."

Remus' face broke into a wide grin. "Is that so? Well, well, well. Isn't that adorable? Are you two going to share a milkshake? One straw or two? One straw means you're going steady. Two straws means he has an STD, but he's afraid to tell you."

Rory's hand went to her forehead. "You're making me

nervous! I only came in here to see if anything could be done about Benjamin."

Remus' face fell. "No, hun. You know the house rules. If you're here, I watch you, but you're Benjamin's charge the second you step out those doors. It was a big ordeal just to get your parents to keep Benjamin out of the building when you first started here, and he still comes and scouts out the perimeter every morning. I'm sorry, but rules are rules. Safety first."

"This stinks!"

"I'll be sure to tell Benjamin you love him."

"Oh, hush. You know what I mean."

He studied her nervous fidgeting, and her need to stand straight as an arrow. "Rory?"

"Yes, Uncle Remus?"

"I want you to tell me everything about your date tonight over dinner. I think it's great you're taking your relationship out into fresh air. Cord is a good guy."

Dread coursed through Rory as she touched her forehead. "That Mexican place just outside of town is nearly empty this time of day, right?"

"That sounds like a safe bet for a first date. You've got your sunglasses and a hat in the car. It'll be fine."

"Thanks." She smoothed the front of her gray blouse, and then leaned over the desk to kiss Remus' cheek. "It'll be fine, right?"

"More than fine. You haven't been on a proper date in ages."

"I DON'T THINK YOU UNDERSTAND THE SEVERITY. HE WAS actually naked, and actually on my bed."

Rory sniggered into her taco salad. "Can't blame a guy for trying. That's some high self-esteem, to use his nude body as a selling point, unsolicited."

"Hilarious. That was the last roommate I had. Since Albert rubbed his junk all over my sheets, I decided I prefer living alone."

"I can't imagine why. Poor Albert. Can you blame him? I mean, you're positively delightful."

"I'm glad you think so." Cordray dimpled at her gentle teasing, and Rory thought to herself what a perfect shade of dark caramel his skin was, and how handsome he was when he laughed. His brown eyes locked in on hers, and for a moment, both of them wished Benjamin wasn't at the table.

When Benjamin rose from his seat, he placed his hand on the center of Rory's spine. "I'll be right back. I need to check that car's plates."

Rory shot him a look of gratitude that he was giving them a moment unsupervised. "He's usually not that lax. He must be starting to trust you. Well done. You even bewitched old Benjamin."

Cord brushed his gloved knuckle against hers, but Rory retracted her hands and tucked them under the table with a look of warning. Cordray tilted his head to the side as he studied her darting eyes and careful movements. "Was this too soon for you?"

Rory kept her voice low, though there were only a handful of other diners in the restaurant. Thanks to her black hat that shrouded a good portion of her face, no one had recognized her. "Things are going so well between us. If something got to be too much and spooked you away..." She shook her head, her voice pinched with worry. "I don't think I could take it."

"I didn't mean to scare you. I just feel like I'm doing this all in the wrong order. I feel like a tool for having never taken you on a date before."

Rory's eyes softened around the edges. "You're wonderful to suggest this. Maybe this is exactly how our first date was always going to go."

"Then have some of your lunch. Can't have my favorite Story going hungry. What would the press say?"

"Oh, shush." Her phone rang in the two-noted chime that was designated for Benjamin. "Sorry, I have to answer when Benjamin calls. Security nonsense."

Cord waved his hand to excuse her apology. "Take it. I totally understand. I have to do the same thing whenever my bodyguard calls."

Rory narrowed her eyes at his teasing. "What's up, Benjamin?"

Her guard's voice sounded tight. "There's a car out here registered to a man who's been dead for five years. Do you see anyone shady in there?"

"No. I'll do a lap and let you know." She hung up and set her phone on the table. "Did you want more water? I'm almost out. I'll go flag down a waiter." Though she didn't need to, she stood and moved to the bar area, asking for a refill so she could survey the restaurant.

When Rory sat back down, she debated taking a chance and reaching across the table to hold his hand. How she wanted to be a woman on a regular date without external complications.

Cord's expression had been lively and mildly flirty just a minute ago, but now it was stony. "You missed a text."

Rory checked her phone and saw a text from Henry, whom she hadn't spoken to in over a week. She still hadn't told him she was seeing Cordray, mostly because she enjoyed the private bubble she had with her boyfriend and wanted to keep it intact as long as she could.

Her lips pulled to the side as she read Henry's message. *"Tell me you love me, and that I own your heart. Take me to the gallery this weekend? We didn't see everything last time."*

Rory texted back a quick, *"Love you to the moon and back. Can't do this weekend. Take one of your many adoring fans."* When she looked up from her phone, she took in the stiffness that flattened Cordray's lips. "Everything alright?"

"You tell me. You're keeping me a secret, while the Prince of Avondale is saying he owns your heart. Am I missing something?"

All the color drained from Rory's face. "What? No!

Henry is my dearest, oldest friend. You know there's nothing going on between us. He's just like that. You know how he is; you're his neighbor."

"I've barely met him more than a handful of times. I'm his neighbor for a property he barely visits, and we mostly keep to ourselves." Cordray shook his head. "I don't get it. He's allowed to ask you on dates to public events, but we're hiding out in no man's land, like you're ashamed to be seen with a Lethal."

Anxiety welled up in Rory as she scooted closer. "Us being here is a big step for me. This is me protecting you. You can't honestly think I'm ashamed of you. I love you!"

It was the first time either of them had said anything like that to each other, and of all the ways Rory envisioned herself speaking those three amazing words, she never heard them being flung out in frustration.

Cordray blinked at her, his mouth open in shock.

Before either of them could speak, Benjamin was beelining toward her with wide eyes. The restaurant was sparsely populated, so when someone bumped into her seat and brushed her shoulder, she took note of the oddity.

Then a sickening wave of heat hit her. It was the kind she sometimes experienced when the flu descended too quickly, and she was hit with an overwhelming urge to lie down before she passed out. As her eyelids drooped, she called out to Benjamin, panicked that someone had Pulsed her with a suggestion of Rest. It was one of those gifts that could go either way. You could use it to help those around you sleep peacefully, or you could force people to pass out against their will, and then take your advantage.

"Run, Cord!" she warned through slack lips, but he didn't listen.

Cordray's chair tipped backward as he lunged around the table to catch Rory before she fell off her chair – a lifeless ragdoll in his arms.

13

SOMEWHERE TO HIDE

Rory fought with her consciousness in the backseat of the town car, jostled in Cordray's arms.

"You killed that guy!" Cordray shouted, his volume uncontrollable in the aftermath.

"I did what I had to. He attacked the Chancellor's daughter. They can't be allowed to get away with that. Now they'll all know that one of their men died trying to attack our family. They won't be so careless next time." Benjamin shook his head. "Broad daylight, too. Man, they're getting desperate."

"Who are 'they'?"

"That's classified."

"What do they want with Rory?"

"Classified."

Cordray growled in frustration. "Come on, Story. Open your eyes. Explain all of this to me."

Benjamin called the mansion with the press of a button, and explained the situation in clipped, coded phrases that didn't answer any of Cordray's multiplying questions. "You need to get The Chancellor and his wife out of there. The palace? Sure. That'll work. We're too far from there, though. It may be that Rory's the only target, but best be cautious and get Stefan and Leah out." Benjamin paused, a shadow falling over his eyes. "I know where to take her that no one will come looking. I'll confirm once we're safe." Benjamin glanced in the rearview mirror at Cordray. "This is your last chance to bail."

"Bail? With an unconscious woman in my arms? You expect me to walk away from this and just leave her in the back of the car?"

Benjamin's usual firmness with strangers dissipated slightly. "You really do care about her."

Cordray glowered at Benjamin. "I'm this close to losing it over here. Tell me what I need to know, so this doesn't happen again. I'm permanent, okay? I should know how to protect her without having to take off my gloves."

Benjamin responded by focusing on the road, still refusing to answer any questions. "I'll tell you this," he said after a full minute of silence, "Rory is bait. Always has been. Whenever someone wants something from the Chancellor, they go after his daughter, because they know her parents would move heaven and earth for her. The mess you stepped in? This is the tip of the iceberg."

"How often does this happen?" Cordray's hold on Rory grew protective as he clutched her to his chest – a limp doll in his arms.

"Whenever there's dissention in the council. A couple times a year maybe; she's only been actually abducted eight times. Though it's usually in the dead of night, and it's an attack on the mansion. To go after her in broad daylight?" Benjamin shook his head, concern weighting his eyebrows. "It's bad. I would send you away, but frankly, I could use an extra pair of hands in case they intercept us on the way to the safehouse."

"Intercept us?" Cordray ducked down, his jaw tight as he tried to shield Rory with the solid mass of his body.

The phone rang throughout the vehicle, and Benjamin shot Cordray a look of warning to shut up when he answered. "Benjamin."

A woman's voice fretted over the phone. "Benjamin, put Rory on. Honey? Honey?"

"Leah, she's alright. She got Pulsed by someone who won't be a problem anymore. She's unconscious, but she'll be fine. Just like the last time."

Leah burst into a fit of tears. "We're headed to King Hubert's palace. When will you be there?"

Benjamin choked the steering wheel, his voice grim. "I'm taking her to Adam's castle. No one will look for her there."

"Adam is horrible! I know Rory thinks he's harmless, but the boy is mentally unstable!"

Benjamin exhaled a small portion of his frustration. "I realize that, but his castle locks down like a fortress. Until we can get to the bottom of who's behind her attack and why, I want Rory safe. They'll look for her at King Hubert's place, so don't let anyone announce that you're arriving. Stay away from the staff. In fact, Prince Henry's got a few chalets you can hole up in while we get to the bottom of this."

Cordray stiffened when he heard Stefan shouting in the background. "I'll not be forced into hiding! We all know the Baron is behind this. The palace is exactly where I'll be heading to hold court with the king and report that, once again, my daughter was attacked! I'll not hide away in some cozy chalet. Benjamin, get my daughter to safety, and I'll handle the rest."

Benjamin rolled his eyes. "Put Pierre on the phone. I'll not argue with you about this again, Stefan. You'll follow protocol, and that's that."

Cordray tried to piece together the bits of Rory's world that made little sense to him, and fit better in the context of a spy novel. Whatever frustrations he'd held over her reluctance to take their relationship public, he began to let go.

She was a flaccid noodle in his arms, but when he moved his cheek to her face, he was overwhelmed with relief that she was still breathing, her shallow in-and-outs calming his heartrate. "Hang in there, Story. I won't leave you."

Cordray held tight to his promise, and to Rory, as Benjamin drove them away from the city. After a few minutes, Benjamin turned down a dead-end road, ignoring the sign, and driving on the dirt when the pavement ended. Cordray didn't ask anything about where they were going, but he knew by the overgrown, craggy path the car teetered down, it couldn't be anywhere good.

14

THE GENEROSITY OF ADAM FONTAINE

"No," a gruff voice said from the other side of the door.

Benjamin banged as if he was in a boxing match with the immoveable wood, his tone spiking with fury. "Hide in there all you want, Adam, but the future Chancellor of Avalon needs somewhere safe to recuperate. You'll open the door for her, so help me!"

"Are all the hotels full? Is there no room at the inn?" Adam replied with too much sarcasm from the other side of the door.

Benjamin was irate. "Rory and Henry are the only people who haven't given up on you! She visits you every month, and you won't even open your doors to her the one time she has a need? You'd let her freeze out here?"

"You're the one who's letting her freeze. There are hotels not ten miles from here."

Cordray frowned at Benjamin for driving them to a "safe" house that appeared more like a gargoyle-bedecked haunted castle. Everything was gray and surly, the statues all over the place looking down at them with a clear message of "get out." The woods they'd driven through were overgrown, the knotted branches twisting in what looked to be painful and unnatural ways. There was an overwhelming ambiance of doom and a life long-since forfeited.

Benjamin wasn't deterred by the gloom, nor the man behind the door. "Adam, you'll open this door right now!"

Adam huffed. "You have a car you can drive her away in. If anyone's going to be responsible for her safety, it'll be the man who's on payroll for such things. Rory's not as delicate as you all seem to think. It's Stefan and Leah who are fragile, going into hysterics every time their daughter breaks a nail."

Benjamin stomped over to the car, took out a wooden bat from the trunk, marched over to the mailbox and swung, knocking the whole thing over in one shot. "Had enough?"

When Adam didn't open the door, Benjamin moved toward the window to the left of the entrance, aiming to break the glass.

"Put that thing down!" Adam bellowed. "How is my castle the place that screams 'safe harbor' to you?"

"Because no one would dare come here and risk having to deal with a spoiled brat like you!" Benjamin lowered the bat and addressed the peephole. "The most likely scenario is whoever ordered the attack on Rory is still out there looking for her."

"And you led them straight to my doorstep?"

Benjamin shot the security camera above the frame a simpering look. "Like you're afraid of anyone. Let us in, or Rory's at risk."

There was a long pause, but finally the lock behind the wood shifted, and the door creaked open two entire inches. "Fine. Keep your paws off the furniture."

Benjamin exhaled so loudly that his shoulders drooped with relief. "Finally." Then he turned his chin to address Cordray in a whisper. "Whatever you do, don't stare.

"What?"

When they moved over the threshold, Cordray didn't need any further clarification. Adam was easily six and a half feet tall, burly, and had firm command over his domineering gait. That wasn't what caused a chill to run up Cordray's spine. Hideous scars that looked akin to a cross between growths and burn marks littered his skin. He was hairy, and the combination of that, plus the growths above his lips which looked almost beastly in nature, made him look like a sideshow medical anomaly.

Cordray had seen photos of Adam in the papers over the years. Everyone knew of the Bachelor of the Year who'd been turned into a hideously deformed monster, but it was a whole different experience to see the owner of

Fontaine Mortgages up close. Cordray took a step back, wanting to run Rory far, far away from the man who looked like he ate small children for breakfast. It would be one thing if the deformities came with a sweet disposition, but Adam looked ready to pounce at the slightest infraction.

"What are you staring at?" Adam growled. It seemed everything he uttered came with a slight guttural roughness to it. He was lionish in nature, and Cord entertained the errant thought that Adam was toying with him the way a jungle cat would before the kill.

Cordray cleared his throat, recalling that he'd never once been intimidated by another man. He postured, looking the beast directly in the eyes. "Where am I taking her?"

"Upstairs. Use any room you like in the East wing. You'll have to forgive the mess. Maid's off-duty." He said it like a joke because it was clear a broom hadn't seen the inside of the gloomy, dusty castle in who knows how long. Then Adam stiffened. "Keep her out of the west wing. That's off-limits." He pointed to the east wing. "Rory usually stays in the first room on the right. Her and Henry."

Cordray knew he shouldn't ask, but he couldn't help himself. "She shares a bedroom with Henry?"

Adam's smile grew sinister at the notion of a wicked game well played as he took in Cordray's curiosity that was paired with the protective way he held onto Rory. "Why, of course. The Prince of Avondale is the one she's betrothed to marry."

Cordray's mouth went dry, though he knew he shouldn't care enough to be baited. Everyone knew about Rory's betrothal to Prince Henry, but the way Adam spoke made it sound like things were still going according to that plan. A wave of jealousy rushed through him, and the candelabra on the curio began to levitate as his frustration grew.

Adam's eyes grew wide with panic at the oddity, and he dove for the golden candelabra. "No! Don't mess with my things. This is far more valuable than you could possibly understand." He clutched the brass to his chest, brushing his hand around the base as if it was his beloved teddy bear.

Benjamin's eyebrows puckered. "How is your magic doing that? You're not due for another pill until next week. Am I wrong on that?" He frowned. "I must've marked my calendar wrong. Your magic's starting to come back, so keep tight inside those gloves."

"What sort of riff-raff is Rory taking pity on this time?" Adam looked Cordray over with a snarl of distaste. "Usually I'm the only man in her life that makes people's skin crawl."

Cordray's upper lip curled at the affront, but he didn't respond. Instead he held Adam's haughty gaze for a few beats before moving past the entryway toward the staircase. Though Rory had been light as a daisy moments before, now she felt heavy, like he was carrying a sack of bricks that didn't belong to him, up the wide and winding staircase. Cordray couldn't even be enchanted by the marble floors or five-foot tall portraits hanging in dusty gold frames. The castle was cobwebby and cold, and he felt the sting of it deep down in his bones. He'd asked out an engaged woman. He was carrying her to the room she'd shared with the actual Prince of Avondale, apparently. Though he should've still felt the worry of the attack, instead he felt hollow. He wanted to trust her, and part of him still did. Even so, his mouth was drawn in a tight line as he moved through the massive home.

He didn't say a word until Benjamin led them to a room that had slightly less dust in it, but still looked unused. When the door shut behind them, Cordray laid Rory on the queen-sized bed. There was something precious and intimate about the act of laying her down. He glanced at Benjamin, who was punching a number into his phone with a worried look on his face. Cordray worried she might get cold, so he lifted Rory up again. This time, he kicked back the dingy seafoam green satin comforter, and laid her down atop the sheets. It was too drafty in the room for her to be uncovered, and the guilty part of Cordray wanted to know what it would feel like to tuck the beauty into bed. He'd never entertained that desire before with a woman, but the longing to do something so matrimonially intimate raged in his veins.

Rory looked like a porcelain doll, laid in the sheets, her

midnight tresses spilling onto the pillow in soft waves. He knew he shouldn't lean over and brush those few stray locks from her forehead, but his hand moved on its own, sweeping her hair as easily as she'd swept him away the first day he'd met her.

Benjamin cleared his throat as he held his phone to his ear, letting Cordray know he had an audience.

Cordray took the comforter clean off the bed and moved into the hallway, shaking the dust off to keep her from having to breathe in anything foul. He didn't look at Benjamin when he reentered and fluffed the green satin over Rory's unresponsive body. The desire to sit on the edge of the bed was strong, but he settled for pulling up a chair next to her and holding onto her hand.

When Benjamin was in between calls, Cordray found his voice. "Prince Henry should be told that she's down for the count."

Benjamin was barely listening, but nodded, motioning to Rory's purse where her phone lay.

Cordray felt like a creeper going through her purse, and plucked out her phone, scrolling through the contacts until "Henry" came up. It took a few steadying breaths, but finally he called the famous man he'd met a few times, since they were technically neighbors in the woods.

The singing voice that greeted him took all hope of levity from the room. "Rory, Rory! Rory, my love. Rory, my dove. Rory, my... something that rhymes with dove. Glove! You're my glove, Rory. My one and only glove. No! *We're* gloves, because we're two of a kind, destined to always be together."

Cordray fought the urge to hang up. "Yeah, this is Cordray Phillips, your neighbor in Helmington Forest."

There was a brief pause, and then recognition flavored Henry's tone. "Ah, yes. Good to hear from you, Cordray. What can I do for you? And how did you come upon Rory's cell phone?"

"Thought you should know Rory was attacked while we were out, and she's unconscious."

The song died off, and Henry's voice grew immediately serious. "What? Is she in the woods now? Who attacked her? Is she alright? She's unconscious? Does Remus know?"

Cordray's face felt stony, his heart thudding in confusion. "I'm not sure if Benjamin's called him, but I can check. We're not in the forest; we're just outside the city. Some friend of hers, Adam, mentioned you, so I thought you should know your fiancée's not doing so hot." He threw out the word to see if Henry would contradict him.

"Rory's at Adam's with you? Adam let in a stranger?"

Cordray was curt. "Whatever. She's safe here with Benjamin and me, so do what you like with that."

The sound of Henry grabbing his keys crackled in Cord's ear. "I'll be there as soon as... Oh, come on. The attack wasn't on me! I should be able to go check on Rory. House arrest? Are you freaking kidding me?" He exchanged a few heated words with someone blocking his way before returning to Cordray. "You're staying there with her? And Benjamin's there?"

"Yeah. Not as good as her fiancé, but we can handle things over here."

Henry let out a noise of frustration. "My guards aren't letting us out of the palace because of the attack on Rory. I'll have my phone on me, though. Call me the moment she wakes up. The very second. I bet Stefan and Leah are worrying themselves sick right now." His voice lowered with palpable dread. "Did she prick herself on a needle?"

Cordray felt cold and hollow inside, knowing in just three short months, Rory would be back in a bed for far more dire reasons. "No. Some guy Pulsed her with a hefty dose of Rest, and she passed out. I still don't totally understand what's going on."

Henry's relief was palpable. "That's good. You'll call me the moment she's awake?"

"Sure." Cordray hung up, unable to listen to the sound of Henry's voice another second. He'd never had a problem with the charismatic prince before, but now each word grated on his last nerve. Henry hadn't contradicted him when he'd referred to Rory as Henry's fiancée. The papers were always reporting something about them getting together, and then breaking up. The betrothal was off, and then there would be photos of him on bended knee before her, with her face in her hands. Cordray had never cared much for celebrity gossip, but in the past couple weeks, he spent easily an hour online, clicking through page after page of journalists editorializing on whether or not the power couple would end up together.

He looked down at Rory's hand in his, studying her dainty fingers as he rubbed off a blue ink smudge on the outside of her little finger. The imperfection was endearing to him.

"Engaged," he whispered, rolling the word around on his tongue to immerse himself in its bitter taste. Cordray ran his thumb over her ring finger, noting the absence of an engagement ring.

When the door burst open, Benjamin frowned at Adam, who walked in without feeling the need to knock. "Get your car out of my driveway."

"Call a tow truck," Benjamin groused.

Cordray listened as the two began to bicker, and surreptitiously removed one of his black gloves. He never took them off unless it was absolutely necessary. He hadn't planned on revealing his true nature ever in the presence of Rory, but when Adam started shouting, Cordray stood, placing himself between Rory and the angry man.

He'd hoped it wouldn't come to this, but when Adam neared the bed, Cord was a live wire, ready to attack. "Back up," he warned the beast in a snarl.

"Telling me what to do will only end badly for you. Get out of the way. This is *my* house and *my* bed, so whoever's resting in it belongs to me."

Though Adam hadn't laid a finger on her, Cordray decided that was all the green light he needed. No matter whose ring would end up on her finger, he knew he couldn't stand idly by while aggression piled up around her. She was too sweet, too gentle. She was too important to the Foundation, and to the whole of Avondale.

She was too important to *him*.

It was a shove – a simple act of aggression that, under normal circumstances, wouldn't have amounted to more than escalating a quarrel. But Cordray was well aware of how very not normal his life's circumstances were.

Though Rory was the one with all the secrets, Cordray had an even bigger one. Pure electricity charged through his palms on command and surged through Adam, thrusting him back with a force far greater than any of them could have anticipated. Had he used two hands, it would have delivered a shot of electricity powerful enough to kill. One hand was for stunning.

Adam shot backward through the exit, banging on the doorjamb before he slammed against the far wall, and then landed with a sickening thud on the floor.

15

THE DANGER OF BEING A LETHAL

Cordray tried not to let the insecurity of dread creep into his pores at exposing himself to the room, but his palms began to sweat when he took in what he'd done. He had a moment of debate where he entertained the idea of bolting out of the castle and changing his name and address. It had been so long since his last episode. Still, he knew he couldn't leave Rory, helpless as she was.

When Benjamin's floored expression finally registered what had happened, he ran to Adam.

"Wait! He might still have a current running through him. Usually wears off within a minute."

Benjamin's mouth was dropped open. "Rory told me you were on the pill!"

Cordray ran his tongue over the outside of his teeth. "I am."

"No, you're not! The pill mutes all your magic. That's the whole point of it, so you aren't capable of doing things like this. You just electrocuted Adam!"

Frustration welled up in Cord, threatening to explode. "The pill doesn't work on me, okay? It takes me down a few notches, but stuff like this still happens."

"This is what you can do with your magic muted?" Benjamin's eyes were wide with incredulity. His hand went over his mouth. "It'll be up to the Chancellor, if you'll be allowed around his only daughter after this. You're the deadliest Lethal I've ever heard of if you did all that while on the pill. Stefan was on the fence about Rory dating a Lethal to begin with. Of course, then he met you and loved you. But still. This might change things."

"Yes, I'm well aware of the stigma that brands all of us as criminals. I know I'm a freak above freaks. No father wants their daughter to date me. If I'd used two hands, Adam would've been dead in the next heartbeat," Cordray croaked, his mouth completely dry.

Benjamin's eyes flicked from side to side as he tried to put the pieces in the proper order. "I've never seen a Pulse like yours. To actually electrocute someone while your magic is muted?"

Cordray didn't mean to let a flicker of vulnerability shine through in his eyes, but it was there nonetheless. "Adam will be fine. He shouldn't have come near Rory, yelling like that." Years of childhood anger and hurt were bubbling up. He'd been so careful for so long. But after only a month of kissing Rory, suddenly he was ready to take his gloves off and go to war at the slightest hint she might not be able to smile at him in the morning.

Benjamin held up his hands in surrender, taking a step forward. "Put a cap on those babies, and we'll get you some help."

"Nothing can help me," Cordray replied, morose. Still, he complied and shoved his black driving gloves back into place, not wanting to electrocute two people in one day. His heartbeat throbbed in his neck, exposing his insecurity and need for people to look the other way on his genetic oddity. "I electrocuted my mother on the pill when I was nine. Buried her right before Christmas. Medication isn't strong enough for me."

It was the confession he hadn't had the nerve to tell Rory. Instead he'd blamed his previous lack of traditional medication for people in his condition on the moral grounds that it muted the rest of his magic – which was no small inconvenience. There were two camps of Lethals: those who wanted the pill to keep their loved ones safe, and those who resented it for muting all of their magic, instead of taking away just the one problem area.

Benjamin moved slowly toward Adam, bending down and searching for signs of life. When Adam's eyes opened, there was a flash of fear, and then the usual surly disposition took him over. He didn't even growl a "thanks" to Benjamin when the guard helped him up. He cracked his neck and flexed his fingers a few times before speaking.

"Since when do you allow Lethals near Rory? I would've thought security would be tighter for the Chancellor's daughter. You're falling down on the job, old man."

Benjamin's lips tightened. "Do yourself a favor and shut up. If I wasn't so shocked at what just happened, I might've been able to enjoy someone finally knocking you down a few pegs." Then his gaze cut to Cordray. "I've got nothing against you, Cord. I actually really like you. But until I give you the all clear, you don't touch Rory again. If you truly do care about her, you won't fight me on this."

"Understood." Cordray hung his head, his shoulders slumping in defeat.

16

CURSES AND COUNTER-CURSES

There were too many troubled thoughts swarming around inside Cordray's head like killer bees for him to pick just one on which to fixate. It left a dull headache in him whenever he tried to turn off all errant magic that radiated from him. It was a thing of luck that he worked from his condo for the most part, and Rory was occupied during most of her days. Still, he didn't mind the headaches he'd endured while pretending his magic was completely muted. Rory felt safe around him if he made it seem like his powers were taken away by the pill, so he gave her the lie if it got them closer together.

The coroner's report had blamed faulty wiring for Anissa Phillips' death. It was a kindness Cordray's father had done to ensure his son stayed protected. It was the first time Cord admitted aloud what he'd done in years, his last time being a tearful plea to his father on his deathbed for forgiveness. Though Cordray had been assured he didn't need the clemency he begged for, his father granted him a full dose of his kind, welcoming forgiveness all the same before he passed away.

Cordray knew that if he wanted to start a life with Rory, she and Benjamin needed to know what she was getting herself into.

"It's quite incredible that your magic can burn through a pill," Benjamin explained from his place next to the door. His hands were in his pockets as he leaned against the wall, watching Cordray shift uncomfortably in the chair at Rory's bedside, while Adam reassembled his bearings in the second chair nearer the door. "Lethals who actually kill people while their abilities are in full swing are rare, but I've never heard of anyone accessing their Lethal powers while on the pill. That's the whole point of the medication!"

"Yet we're all treated like we're about to go on a murdering spree, even if we're properly medicated." There weren't many objects in the room, but the few items suspended midair around him, trumping up the menace that swirled inside his heart. There was no point in giving himself a headache anymore by attempting to control his magic. "I'm not dangerous. I wear my gloves and, apart from just now, I never take them off." His eyes cut to Benjamin. "I would never hurt her."

Benjamin's voice was quiet with weight. "I know that. I also know that the Chancellor's going to have something to say about this."

The room was quiet as Adam and Benjamin studied Cordray as he watched Rory. "What's your Pulse?" he asked both men.

Adam snorted. "None of your business. I've already given you space in my castle, and I regret it very much. You don't need to go poking around in my private life."

Benjamin shot Adam a withering look. "Don't listen to Adam; he's always in a mood about something."

"Yes, being electrocuted puts me in the cheeriest of dispositions," Adam droned.

Benjamin shifted his weight from one foot to the other. "My Pulse works sort of like a filter, rather than pressing impulses into people. I can read false intentions. I touch a person, and if they're trying to deceive me, I can feel that."

"Like a human lie detector?"

"Exactly."

Cordray swallowed. "That sounds pretty useful in your profession. Bet you're wishing you'd Pulsed me in the beginning to see if the pill would actually work on me."

Benjamin shifted against the wall, his arms moving to cross over his chest. "Yes, well, had that even been a possibility I'd known to question, I would have.

Cordray's mouth tightened. "I only Pulsed Adam because he looked like he was going to attack Story."

"Who?"

Cord grimaced that he'd let her nickname slip. He jerked his chin at the lifeless girl on the bed. He looked away, embarrassed that he'd let himself attach so easily to her, when he was layered with so many deadly secrets. Not that he could have resisted the pull she had on him. If he was being honest with himself, not even the fact that she might still be engaged to Prince Henry registered a retreat in his mind. He'd never felt as calm and settled as he had when sitting next to her on the couch after their dinners together every night.

Cordray cleared his throat and leaned forward, his elbows on his knees. "I don't go around hurting people at random."

Adam stood and paced the room as he took it all in, listening to Benjamin go back and forth with Cordray on how best to secure Rory's safety, and interjecting when necessary. His gait had slumped off-kilter after the painful shock, but he didn't complain. On the contrary, it seemed that whenever Cordray apologized for the attack, Adam only grew more surly. "Rory is my oldest friend. Of course I'd never harm her. But don't apologize for defending her from what you thought would be an assault. Apologies make men look weak."

Cord couldn't help but spout back, "I'm sorry you feel that way."

Adam stiffened at the sass, but instead addressed

Benjamin. "You're certain she didn't prick her finger? She should've been awake by now."

Benjamin moved to the window, staring out at the autumn leaves falling on the vast expanse of overgrown land as he spoke. "Cordray saw the whole thing. The man didn't have a needle. He Pulsed her."

"Then why isn't she awake?" Adam growled, a low rumble vibrating his chest.

Benjamin kept his eyes on the red, yellow and orange leaves that were falling on the tall shrubbery designed to keep the world out. He noticed Adam's wince when a wolf's howl sliced through the quiet, but didn't address his flinch. "The position of Chancellor is a coveted seat. King Hubert holds only slightly more power than Rory's father. The king even has to consult the Chancellor before he enacts new laws. It's a system of checks and balances that's fragile, but it works. There have been countless failed attacks on the two men, so oftentimes the miscreants refocus their attacks on Rory." He let out a heavy sigh that filled the room with a weight of sadness for the state of the darker parts of the world. "That means Prince Henry's security needs tightening, as well."

Cordray nodded. "That's what I've been thinking. If they can't get to the Chancellor, then they'll pick off the next generation of rulers."

Benjamin nodded. "Malaura would love to get her hands on you. Rory was smart to keep your relationship private. Once Malaura knows you exist?" He shook his head.

Adam didn't hold back his growl. "I don't need any talk of her in my house. Her name has done enough damage to me." Then he turned his head over his shoulder and spoke through gritted teeth at the golden candelabra that he'd brought in to rest on the end table. "I told you to shut up. They don't need to know about that." Then he paused, as if listening to a voice that Cordray and Benjamin could not hear. "It's nobody's business but mine."

Cordray's eyebrows rose, but he didn't say anything about Adam addressing a brass candelabra as if it was a person. The thing was two feet tall, and bespoke of old wealth.

Benjamin cast Cordray a covert look to be cool, confirming that yes, Adam was a very ill man in ways that weren't fixable by plastic surgery. He cleared his throat and continued, turning his attention back to the snow that fell several stories below. "Malaura always wanted more influence, so she dipped into the database of Lethals who'd registered to take the pill, gathering them to herself to form a sort of army. What power she lacked, she made up for with force, acquiring people who could outperform the others. It's why she chose Remus to be her protégé, even though he's not a Lethal. He understands things about magic better than anyone. Lucky for him that he got out from under her thumb when he was still young."

Adam paced in circles around the room, shooting Rory

looks of concern as the minutes ticked by. "But the old witch forgot one thing. We run on a democracy. She was voted out of office, and her more violent followers were locked up. If I had to guess, I'd bet that it's her people behind Rory's attack."

"Everyone thought that when her brother Hubert was voted in, all those problems would go away. He's a good man."

Cordray couldn't take his eyes off of Rory. "But we still have Lethals who are drumming up the stigma all of us get branded with. So all of us pay the price, living in our cabins in the woods, and keeping away from daughters with fathers who love them."

"The kingdom's been mostly at peace ever since, though Malaura's always out there in the shadows, planning who knows what. There's the occasional attack, but that's to be expected." Benjamin moved over to the bed to check on Rory, prying up her eyelids before he gave her a paternal kiss on the forehead. "Everyone assumed Malaura would go away after she was voted out. She murdered twelve guards when she came back at the kingdom-wide celebration that happens whenever the king or the Chancellor have a baby. Rory was a month old when Malaura cursed her, and she's carried that weight ever since."

When it seemed Benjamin was unable to continue, Adam finished the dreaded tale, his words clipped. "On the child's twenty-fifth birthday, she'll prick her finger and die.' Not exactly a lullaby, but that's what Rory got from Malaura." Adam flinched when the evil ex-queen's name escaped his lips. "And I said we weren't going to talk about her in my home!" Adam whirled on Cordray, his anger coming out in what was almost a roar. "You've brought nothing but disaster into my house!"

Benjamin crossed the room and popped the flat of his hand to the beast's chest. "Sit down, Adam. We get it; you're angry at the world. Don't take it out on the new guy." Then Benjamin addressed Cordray with sadness shining in his eyes.

Benjamin rubbed his forehead, wishing the trail didn't end where he saw it all heading. "After Malaura doled out her curse, Rory's uncle did something incredible for her. Remus loves his brother so much that he sacrificed five years of his lifespan to issue out a counter to Malaura's curse. It's hard to enact a counter-curse, but Remus is just that powerful. He was only twelve years old, and he was able to find a way to give us some hope."

Cordray wanted to pace the room, but he knew any sudden movements would make the men uneasy. "I know all of this, and none of it scared me away. Instead of dying, Remus twisted the curse so that Rory will prick her finger on her twenty-fifth birthday, and fall into a deep, unshakable sleep – not unlike the one she's in now." Then to her, he whispered quietly, "Come on, Story. Wake up already."

Benjamin ran his hand over his face. "If the only antidote to her impending coma wasn't true love's kiss, I would have sent you away the second I learned you were Lethal. I'm not sure which is more dangerous at this point – you, her curse, or the fact that you might be the only cure for her curse."

Cordray flexed his fingers a few times, looking down to keep his thoughts private. "I haven't said that to her yet. It's only been a month." Though as he said it, he felt the sting of falsity on his tongue. The words were there, but logic made him tuck them back inside.

Adam snorted dismissively. "I'll never understand our society's obsession with love."

"I'm sure you don't," Benjamin retorted. "Love is the only thing that can unravel the hate it takes to come up with a curse. Remus' counter-curse was strategic. At twelve years old, he understood things about the world that most of us will never grasp."

Cordray moved his chair closer to Rory's bedside, making eye contact with Benjamin to silently tell him that he wasn't going to touch her without permission, but he'd tolerated just about all he could of the distance between them.

"Careful," Benjamin warned, though he didn't move to separate them further.

"She'll be fine. I won't touch her. Now that I know what to look for, I can guard her better when we're out and about."

Adam rolled his eyes. "I wouldn't leave him alone with her, unless you want to be guarding royal babies in nine months. He's a heartbeat away from coupling with her right in front of us."

Cordray was about to bite back with an acerbic retort, but suddenly nothing else in the world mattered, because Rory began to stir.

17

CAFFEINATED KISSES

Though most were intimidated by Adam and gave in to whatever he wanted, Cordray shoved the man aside so he could help Rory through her first moments of wakefulness. He leaned over the bed, casting aside Benjamin's command that he wouldn't touch her. The moment her eyelids fluttered, he knew he didn't have the self-control to step back. He was gentle with her, holding her hand and lifting it to his cheek. It was an intimate touch, and one they'd done many times before when they were alone. Cordray needed to be near her, to ease some of the pain life had heaped on her lovely head. "Hey, Story. What's your Rory?" he asked with a small smile that was meant just for her. Though he still had questions about her attacker, and the dangerous nature of her title, her needs came first.

"What? Are we... I don't..." She blinked hazily until her

eyes finally were able to focus on his – bright brown pools that shone only for her. "Cord," she breathed, and the sound was laced with relief at the sight of his face.

Benjamin threw his arms in the air. "Well, that didn't last long. So much for you keeping your distance."

Cordray held himself back for two whole seconds. Three. Four. On the fifth, he decided she was cogent enough to be able to push him away if his advances were unwanted. Slowly and with so much longing, he could scarcely be parted from her a moment longer, Cordray closed the breath of a gap between them. He lifted her under her torso a few inches, and gently brushed his lips to hers.

Her lips were soft, and after the shock wore off, moved easily with his – as if they'd been kissing for years, but were still enjoying the fruits of their first time. Cordray moved slowly, knowing she was something to be cherished instead of conquered and kept. But he wanted to keep her – to himself, safe, and in his arms.

He let out a vulnerable bleat when her hand rose clumsily to touch on his cheek. Every time she touched him, it roused an exposed nerve that came from living a life so isolated from society. The need for her touch burned raw inside of him, so he leaned in, silently begging for more – ever more. Neither of them cared that they had a stunned audience. They were entranced that something so magical had happened to them.

When his tongue lightly swept across hers, Rory's legs

curled up under the satin comforter, her body responding far easier to him than either of them would've thought possible so soon after her eyelids opened. She arched her back as his kiss sent sensation to the muted parts of her, awakening her senses and making them both crave more.

Soon she was sitting up on her own in the bed. His kiss was like caffeine to her system – rousing her and focusing her foggy mind. When Adam and Benjamin slipped out to give them some privacy, Rory tugged on Cordray's collar, giving in to the longing that never went away. They dedicated that slice of time to exploring, to unwinding, and to playing. The world slowed, and for a few precious and blissful moments, there was only them, and only this kiss.

Cordray didn't know how or why he could be expected to resist the pull she had on him. Finally allowing himself to give in to the desire he'd been tucking away for the past two hours felt like the first breath he'd ever had. Cordray inhaled the sweet, subtle fragrance of her hair as he lightly tugged on the raven waves that had enticed him at every turn. He didn't mean to bite down on her lip, but the sensation only pushed them further and further past the point of no return.

The kiss came to a crest when Rory swooned, her heart working hard to keep up with her libido. She went limp in his arms, though she didn't go completely under.

Cordray laid her back down and kissed her forehead, sitting on the edge of the bed next to her. "Easy, easy. Are you alright? I'm sorry. That was all me."

Rory's lashes fluttered as she held on to consciousness. "Cord," she whispered, her voice falling softly around them. Then as her world came more into focus, she glanced around the room with a frown. "Why are we here?" Then her eyes widened when it dawned on her that there was no way he could be at Adam's haunted castle and not have been introduced to the mentally unstable man. "Whatever Adam said, I apologize. He can be... He's not well."

Cordray responded by leaning over and stroking her lips with his, too sedated by their kiss to care about much else.

18

TWO PILLS, TWO RULERS

It was a week of Benjamin sticking close to Rory's side, but eventually the usual mania that followed an attack came to a crest. Benjamin's team identified the aggressor as Benedict Freeman - a man who'd been dead for five years.

"Clearly the man stole Mr. Freeman's identity, which puts us at square one as far as tracking down whoever ordered the attack on you. I'm too old to assume he was acting on his own. The threat isn't neutralized simply because he's dead." Benjamin was matter-of-fact, while the other guards in the household had been reassuring to the point of making up outright lies to pacify Rory's mother.

Leah Johnstone was in a state in the wake of her daughter's abduction. She attended her daughter's lessons, and even rode with her alongside Benjamin to drop her off at work. After one tutoring session with Tyren, Leah ruled him unsuitable for instructing her daughter. She fired him, handing the reins of her daughter's education back to her brother-in-law.

Studying under Remus was far less stressful for Rory, even with her mother watching. Cordray had been taken into the fold once Benjamin had informed Remus of the above and beyond magic of which the man was capable. Remus was enthralled at the prospect of tutoring someone so naturally gifted, a giddy gleam dancing in his eyes whenever he uncovered a new layer of Cordray's abilities.

"Uncle Remus, I'm certain I'm standing incorrectly." Rory frowned, embarrassed at her lack of ability. It had been years for her, and the china cup had never budged. She'd made her peace with her limitations over the course of her life, but now that her boyfriend had been brought into her sessions, it renewed a competitive drive in her she'd long put aside.

Remus moved next to her and adjusted her gait. "You're standing just fine. Hey, don't beat yourself up. You're back with me now. Tyren isn't here to run you down simply because you're fallible, like the rest of us."

"There's fallible, and then there's failing. In front of my boyfriend, no less." Her voice lowered, adding a tightness to her facial muscles.

Remus tapped his finger under her chin, which was prone to drooping when she was caught in melancholy.

"Cordray is gifted. No matter who he's studying with, he would outperform them."

"Stop being gracious and logical. Call me a child and have done with it."

Remus touched her nose, as he'd done when she was little. "You're being a child. So you have limitations. We all do."

She shot him a dubious glare. "Name five of yours."

"I'm far too handsome, far too gracious, my magic is sometimes too powerful, I'm too wealthy, and..." He looked up at the ceiling, and then shrugged. "I'm afraid I can't think of a fifth fault that I have."

Rory sniggered. "You're impossible today. Whenever you get around Cord, you get all goofy. You love that you finally get a student who challenges you."

Cordray glanced up from the book he was studying titled "Timeless Spells for Timebound Magicians". "It's fine, Story. I run circles around you in the kitchen, too. Get used to staring at my sweet backside." Cordray turned a page and began scanning it. "What does it matter if you're better than me at some things, and I'm a little ahead of you at others? Isn't that how a good team works? Plus, you know all this stuff – in Latin, no less. It's only a matter of time before your body catches up with your brain."

Remus gave her a book to study while he went over his notes with a zealous glow as he sat at his desk. Rory watched her uncle organize the lesson plans for two vastly different levels of ability, never looking ruffled or impatient with her. His boyish fascination with the unusual was triggered at working with Cordray. The promising student learned everything so quickly, and performed each task with mastery. Rory knew her uncle well enough to know that working with Cordray had given Remus hope that perhaps there were still things out there that could surprise him. He'd been sought after by many gifted students for tutoring, but had turned them down so he could protect her. That she'd brought someone so uniquely talented to his doorstep was just the treat he'd been longing for, so she felt slightly mollified that if she couldn't be the star pupil, she could at least usher one into the study.

When the door opened near the end of their session, the Chancellor strolled in with a politeness to his tight smile. "I see you're all hard at work. The snow is really coming down out there. I think you two might want to wrap it up for the night."

The fatherly air of "get the crap away from my daughter" was tamed by the "I don't want my sweet girl to die alone," but still made for slightly awkward interactions between Cordray and the Chancellor. Rory's father had been slightly more on-edge after learning that the pill that helped them all sleep better at night only took Cordray's abilities down a couple notches, instead of muting them altogether. While most fathers went through the dance of learning how to gracefully handle suitors when their daughters turned teenagers, Rory's social standing was such that the screening process to get a date with her left precious few to throw their hats into the mix, and those were often deterred by taking one look at Benjamin.

Cordray stood and stretched, and then offered his hand to the Chancellor. "Thank you for letting me study with Remus, sir."

Stefan took Cord's gloved hand, and then reached into his pocket. "I almost forgot. Your additional medication came in today." He presented Cordray with a bottle that held only a single pill rattling around inside. "Take this with the other still in your system, and let's see if it takes away your magic for thirty days. I know there are downsides to muting one's magic, and if you were seeing any other woman in the land, perhaps you could go off the pill altogether and just rely on your gloves. But seeing as you're dating the future Chancellor of Avondale, safety comes first. I hope you understand."

"Yes, sir. Couldn't agree more."

Rory let out a breath she hadn't realized she'd been holding. Cordray had every right to refuse just the one pill, but to take two? No one had ever tried that before, nor had they needed to. That Cordray saw the man behind the council chair and didn't flinch away from the hard line put her mind at ease that not only would he do anything to keep her safe, but he would also do anything to keep the peace with her parents.

The Chancellor's eyes fixed on the bottle, as if he was addressing it instead of the man before him. "Though I'm sure it seems cruel to you to take away all your magic, it was a long road to get to this point. In the medieval times, there was torture and all kinds of deprivation therapy to try and 'cure' the Lethals of their desire to harm others with a solitary touch. Of course, we now know that's preposterous. People can control their desire to do harm, but they can't control what their Pulse is. Nature does what it does, and we do what we do – those are two separate things." He looked Cordray up and down with a note of fatherly advice to him. "I can see what kind of man you are by the fact that you wear these gloves, and only invoked your Pulse to defend my daughter. Admirable."

"Thank you, sir."

"Stefan, Cordray. Call me Stefan."

Cord shook the pill into his gloved hand, and his voice came out tremulous. "Listen, I care about your daughter, and I know that probably makes me someone you don't like all that much. But I straight up love you, man. If I take this, I can't hurt her?"

Stefan's eyes narrowed in on Cordray with kindness that was laced with a subtle hint of a threat. "You will never, ever harm my daughter."

Rory and Remus looked on as Cordray downed the pill, their matching expressions of hope lighting up the room brighter than any manmade illumination ever could. Rory had been focusing on the unfair side effect of losing his magic; she hadn't counted on him not caring about that loss as much anymore, if it meant he could touch her skin without a barrier between them.

"How long does it take to kick in?" Cord asked, his eyes on Rory with unconcealed longing.

"Should only take an hour or so before it's in your system and working at its full effect. I appreciate your caution."

"Then I'll be going." He shook Stefan's hand again, but instead of leaving his gratitude at that, he pulled the older man in for a tight hug. "Thank you."

Though Rory could tell Stefan wanted to resist Cord, she loved her father for clutching her boyfriend tighter, offering acceptance Cordray didn't often get. Stefan patted Cordray on the back a few times, unable to keep the paternal smile off his face. "Think nothing of it, Son." Then he watched Cordray pack up his things and head for the door. "Do you have plans for the weekend at the end of the month?"

"No, sir."

"I'm going to be taking my family to go skiing a week after Aurora's birthday. Would you like to join us?" With a twinkle in his eyes, he added. "With you in the picture, I'm planning for Malaura's curse to be defeated within the hour my daughter should fall ill. I'm making all sorts of plans for the week after Malaura is made a public fool, showing the kingdom that her brand of hatred has no place in the land."

Remus' shoulders rolled back. "I love that sentiment. Malaura hates it when she fails, all the more when it happens publicly." Then he met his niece's eyes. "And make no mistake, her curse will fail."

Cordray nodded with a flood of warmth at being invited in on a family vacation, but Rory frowned at her father. "We have a council meeting that weekend."

Stefan inhaled slowly as he stood straight, donning a tired smile as he looked on his pride and joy. "Change of plans. I'm considering taking on a partner who can run things, so I can take the occasional weekend away with my family. The Baron suggested it, and I think it's a good idea."

"What?" Rory screeched, forsaking her ladylike decorum for indignation. "Please tell me you're joking."

"I'm quite serious, and quite through talking about it. This was my decision, no matter what you might think."

Rory's hands balled into fists, and she glanced at Remus, who looked equally shocked. "They're using my curse to force your hand to give up some of your authority! Tell me it's any different, and I'll let it go." When Stefan merely looked away, Rory's nostrils flared. "That's what I thought."

A wave of exhaustion seemed to come over Rory's father, painting his eyes with pain he didn't bother to conceal. "Do you truly think I'd cower to the Baron? I'm tired of it, is what's happened. My daughter's been abducted for the last time! Let someone else deal with malicious malcontents attacking their child to try and make us comply. I belonged to you and your mother long before I belonged to Avondale. It's not the Baron forcing my hand, it's me handing over part of my authority so I can be a better father. I wanted a better life for you than this."

Rory shook her head, her voice tight with emotion. "Dad, this isn't the way."

"It's my way, and it's not up for discussion." Stefan turned to Cordray. "We'll see you tomorrow after work for more tutoring. Always a pleasure, Cordray."

"This isn't over," Rory warned her father.

The moment Cordray exited, Stefan held up his hand to stave off Rory. "Enough. This is my decision. You're my daughter, and I'll not let you concern yourself with things I'm to take care of. It wasn't until you took up with a Lethal, and I was actually happy to have the extra protection around you, that I realized how very backwards I've been doing things."

Remus' eyes were narrowed in anger. "Stefan, Rory will never be out of danger. Think about it; the people who've abducted or attacked her have never asked for ransom. It's never been about the money."

"Exactly! It's about my position, and I'll not let it be a danger to my family any longer." He rubbed the creases across his forehead, his shoulders slumping. "King Hubert and I had a discussion about what might happen if you don't wake up."

Rory's mouth went dry. "That seems like a conversation I should've been present for."

Stefan made no apologies. "You're the heir to the head seat on the council. If you're in your coma, and something happens to me, then what? Who will run the council? It will fall to chaos, and you know it."

Remus shook his head. "No. We'll think of another option than you choosing the Baron as your co-chair. No ruler at all would be better than him, and I can say the same for his snake of a son. Put this decision off, Stefan. You're acting out of fear. If Rory manages to escape her curse..."

Rory's head snapped in her uncle's direction. "*If*? *If* I manage to escape the curse?"

Remus shrank, and held up his hands. "I misspoke. When. *When* you put Malaura's curse to shame, you'll be sought after even more."

"Actually, it'll be you everyone's buzzing about, since you'll have been the one to overthrow her curse by casting the counter-curse to begin with."

Remus inclined his head to her. "Ah, but people are afraid of me. They'd never try to attack me."

Rory's mouth set in a hard line. "Right. And I'm just a stupid Deadpulse."

Her father stiffened, but Remus pointed his finger in his niece's face. "There's about three things wrong with that sentence. Rethink yourself, Rory."

Rory had plenty of things to say on the subject, but she

kept the bulk of them to herself. Stefan left the room and retired to his bedchambers, so he could toss and turn, as the rest of the household did that night.

19

NEGOTIATING WITH CALVIN

Cordray held up his hands, as if that was the measure of masculine attractiveness. It was his first day without gloves, and he was loving the freedom. Every little brush of his fingers against Rory's was a heightened sensation that almost made him choke up with how long he'd waited to feel anyone's skin. Rory was soft, delicate, and the best reward for going twenty-nine years of hardly touching anyone. She was preoccupied, though, when he thought she'd be celebrating his newfound freedom. He loved the feel of Rory's silky skin, and longed for her to finish up with the workload, so he could take her out to lunch.

He'd been waiting in his car at noon in the parking lot to take her to lunch, as he'd done every day that week, but she was running late. She buzzed him up, taking the first baby step at letting him into her world via her office.

Of course, no one paid much attention, as she had meetings scheduled on and off all throughout the day all the time. But still, their eyes danced at each other with the thrill of secrecy as he took the seat across from her at her desk, waiting patiently while she finished up a call from a contractor.

The moment she hung up, her phone rang again. "I'm so sorry, Cord. It's been nonstop today."

"I'm in no hurry."

"I've got to take this call. Would you mind waiting in here for a few minutes?"

Cordray studied her squirrely movements, and then nodded. "No problem. Take your time." His eyes flicked to the phone's screen, reading her Caller ID. "Who's 'Arrogant Prat'?"

Rory held the phone to her chest, as if that might undo his memory of who was calling. "No one you'll ever have to meet, fortunately. Not a good guy. I'll be right back."

Cordray's eyebrows pulled together. His first instinct was to follow her to see what shady characters were calling her, but he knew that wouldn't make for a great show of trust. Still, he sat on the edge of his seat, anxious for her to return.

～

WHEN RORY MOVED QUICKLY THROUGH THE OFFICE TOWARD the empty breakroom, she kept the conversation quiet. "Calvin, thanks for returning my call."

"Of course. How's my little Roar doing these days?"

Rory grimaced. "I need a favor. I want an unofficial meeting with the council elders, but without my dad."

"Ah. This is about your father's decision to split the head Council seat."

"Of course. Do you think there's a way to undo it?"

Calvin sighed heavily. "Not if he was the one to suggest it. It's his chair to do with as he wishes."

"You know this is fishy!"

"Honestly, why do you even care? Your family will be able to keep their fortune even if your father retires, which isn't even happening. He's merely splitting the responsibility because it's clearly too much for him to handle." Then he seemed to catch himself in the logic, though Rory could tell he'd puzzled everything out on his own. "Ah, but that would mean any future contributions to your family fortune would be split in two. My, my. That is a problem. My father seems the most likely candidate for the number two position, since he's got the most seniority. That would put your father and mine on equal footing, which means..."

Rory cringed. "When they pass down their seats, they would go to you and me. We would co-rule together."

A slow laugh bubbled to the surface, making Rory's upper lip curl. "Far easier than us getting married, isn't it?"

"That will never happen."

"Oh, little Roar. It's already happening. There's no undoing what the Chancellor sets into motion. He only has to name his companion, and the way the council is run will change forever. I should think the people will be relieved. Now when the regime is passed down to us, there won't be only a Deadpulse making all the decisions."

Rory paled. "You and I have completely opposing political views. Nothing would ever get accomplished."

"I'm sure we could do all sorts of things together," he said with a smarm to his tone that made Rory clutch her cardigan tighter around her shoulders. "Long nights spent in heated debate just the two of us? I can practically see the sex tapes surfacing already."

Rory wrestled with the urge to shout at Calvin. "My father should be able to keep his seat without having to share it. The council can thrive, as it's always done under his rule."

"I can't imagine how tiresome it must be to care as much as you do. You can try all you like, but you know the Baron. Once he's got his mind set on something, that's the way it plays out."

Rory wanted to scream at Calvin, but she kept her voice even. "Then I look forward to a lifetime of voting you down."

"Whatever you like, birthday girl. Are you frightened, now that the date for your curse is coming due?" Calvin spoke with an overly dramatic vibrato to his voice.

Rory swallowed hard. "Frightened people hide themselves away. You know very well I gave up hiding from my fate the moment I learned to walk on my own."

"Do you think it'll happen at 12:01 on your birthday? Tales of woe are always sexier when they're carried out at the stroke of midnight."

Rory shuddered. "Don't say 'stroke'. It sounds creepy coming from you."

Calvin laughed as she hung up. Rory didn't waste any time calling the next number on her list. "Henry! I've called you five times today. Where have you been?"

It sounded to Rory like Henry was walking down an echoy hallway, and she guessed he was in his palace. "If it isn't my future bride, all eager to hear the sultry sound of my voice. What can I do for you, baby?"

Rory's shoulders relaxed at his goofball flirting that was never serious. "I need a favor. Being that you're my future husband, I'm sure you'll have no problem doing my bidding."

"A dozen roses? Done! But why stop there? A dozen chariots with a dozen horses for my future bride. I'll put in the order today. Happy almost uncurse day to you, my love."

"Why, thank you, kind sir. About that favor."

"I hardly think now is the appropriate time to walk you through phone sex. I'm horribly out of practice. It's been five, six hours since my last over-the-phone tryst with some desperate young lovely."

"Would you shut it? Listen, I need you to talk to your father, and convince him that my dad shouldn't split his ruling seat with anyone."

Rory could hear the frown in Henry's voice. "That sounds nothing at all like phone sex."

"I'll talk you off all day long if you can put your Pulse of Charm to good use and get my dad to see reason."

"You will?"

She managed a small smile. "Not a chance. Go find one of your usual desperate young lovelies, and enjoy necking in your neck of the woods."

Henry's voice dropped with a note of seriousness. "Are you sure we shouldn't hedge our bets with two Chancellors? This way, if you take a long time coming out of your coma, the kingdom won't be in a state of panic – other than the fact that they'll miss your lovely face, of course."

"Can you picture Calvin being your number two? Because that's what we're dealing with, Henry."

She could picture Henry's grimace at the prospect of being stuck in a lifetime of fruitless meetings with the weasel they both despised. "Fair point. I'll see what I can do." His voice lightened back to its original buoyancy. "I really did get you a birthday gift, and it's even better than a dozen red roses."

Rory smiled, now that the task was off her plate. "You did?"

"But you can't open it until the day after your actual birthday, because that's how sure I am that your curse won't hold water. And if it does, you'll be so motivated to wake up to open my gift, you'll reduce the lengthy coma to a six-hour nap, just so you can open my present."

Rory brightened by degrees at Henry's perpetual boyish cuteness, cradling the phone to her ear with a sweetness to her movements that came whenever her favorite friend doted on her. She started refilling the coffee in the pot for her employees as she spoke. "I love you, Henry. Thank you. You're the best prince a girl could ask for."

"I totally am. Love you, too. Next time I see you, I'll have a big, sloppy kiss ready and waiting for you, wowing the crowd with our torrid affair. They'll forget all about your curse or any political nastiness when rumors of us running off into the sunset circulate again."

Rory chuckled at his antics. "Will you wear lipstick this time? I feel like we need to up the controversy. We've led far too dull of lives thus far."

"Absolutely. Couldn't agree more. This last attacker didn't even abduct you! They're losing their touch."

Henry had done his grand sweeping princely kiss with her several times. It was always in public, and he always tried to slip his gum in her mouth because he said that made it all seem all the more tawdry for the viewers.

"I'll see you later, Prince Charming."

"Counting the minutes, my love," Henry said before hanging up.

It was the eve of her twenty-fifth birthday, which

caused her no small amount of anxiety. She didn't want to lose her sanity by dwelling on Malaura's curse, but the dread was there all the same. Everyone had urged her to take the day off of work, but somehow to Rory that felt like conceding defeat to Malaura, which she was unwilling to entertain.

"Who was that?" asked Cordray. She realized when she turned that he was standing stone-faced behind her.

"Just a friend. Hopefully you'll meet him at my birthday party." Her parents had spared no expense, planning a celebration in defiance of Malaura's curse to take place the week after her birthday. The affair was more the middle finger to everyone in the kingdom who'd ever reminded them that Rory wasn't supposed to live to see her twenty-fifth year. More RSVPs than ever before were coming in, everyone eager to see the outcome. The caterer had even mentioned that the menu could easily shift to a mourning spread, in case things went south and never bounced back for the Chancellor's daughter. Leah and Stefan had been none too pleased about that little anecdote.

Cordray was not pacified with her canned response. "How long have you loved Henry?"

THE CHAOS AND KISS OF PRINCE HENRY

Despite the fact that it was chilly outside, Rory tugged Cordray out the back exit, so they could speak privately. "Prince Henry is my oldest friend. You know that."

"I don't have any oldest friends who I talk to like that."

"Well, you can speak to Henry in the same way. He'll love it." She sighed. "Henry and I would never have worked. He's wonderful, but he's got a wandering eye, and can't commit to a dinner order, much less a woman. Trust me, this is how it was supposed to be. He's going to be the king someday, and I'll be the Chancellor. It's good that we work well together and have a silly friendship."

She shivered, and Cordray glanced around the empty alley behind the building before wrapping his arms around her. "Say more things that make me forget how sexy and teasing you sounded on the phone to him."

"Henry, Adam and I didn't have many friends who understood the expectations that were put on us from birth, so the three of us clung to each other. But nothing romantic ever came of it."

"Maybe I'll feel better once the three of us hang out."

Given Henry's handsome face and flirty nature, Rory very much doubted that.

Cordray took a chance and kissed her, shivering as the light fluffs of snow began to fall around them. Fall had given way to the beginnings of winter, making everything seem quieter, as if nature herself was growing more contemplative. "Where can I take you for lunch? I was hoping to steal you away to our favorite secret spot." They hadn't been outed by the press yet, and Rory was grateful for the time they had that was uninterrupted by the demands of the people.

"You want to steal me?" She lifted up onto her toes and pecked his lips. "But I'm already yours."

"I want to steal you and keep you." He kissed her several more times, warming them in the midst of the chilly gusts coming in from the left end the alley. "Mine," he whispered between kisses, his palms moving along the gentle curve of her back.

"Yours," she cooed, letting herself get weak in the knees for him. They felt scandalous, indulging when any number of her employees could pop out back for a smoking break and uncover their relationship. "We're always around other people," she complained, and then snatched his lower lip between hers, drawing it out just to make him moan for her. "I've been loving this time that's just ours."

"Tonight it'll be just you and me." His hand gravitated to her hip, running down the slope of it so he could grip her thigh possessively.

"And Benjamin," she reminded him as the kiss came to a crest.

"Right." Cordray pressed his forehead to hers. Words of permanence sizzled on the tip of his tongue, but he bit them back, not wanting to admit them to her at the office. "Tell me again your curse will be easily defeated."

"As fast as you can kiss me, I'll be back in your arms."

His soft reply had the hint of pride to it at having captured her heart so thoroughly. "Right where you belong."

"After I wake up, my parents are taking us on a fun weekend of skiing. Then there's the big celebration when we get back, where you'll meet everyone."

"Meet everyone as what?"

Rory frowned, confused. "As yourself, of course."

"As your boyfriend?"

Rory's mouth drew to the side, anticipation lighting her face with joy. "I think we can go public at my birthday party, if you're up for it."

Cord beamed as he kissed her, triumphant at the label he'd been trying not to push. "We could go public now, you know. Walk in there with your skirt all askew and my shirt unbuttoned, holding hands for everyone to see. They wouldn't gossip about you and Henry anymore, that's for sure."

"After my birthday," she insisted with a snigger. She couldn't resist kissing him again. Most of their time together was spent with Remus or Benjamin as a third wheel, which put a serious damper on any kind of romance.

They walked back inside, their hands parting for the sake of keeping things quiet. They were shivering, but content that they'd taken a moment for themselves. Cordray put his hand on the small of her back as they neared her office, and she shot him a look that said she knew he was trying to subtly plant their relationship in the minds of their coworkers.

He returned her squint with an innocent shrug. "What?"

"You know what you're doing," she said out of the corner of her mouth. "I'll see you in there in a minute. I have to check something with my graphic artist. Then we can go, I promise."

"Take your time." Cordray moved into her office and sat back down without a hint of frustration at having to wait.

Rory stood beside her employee's desk, ignoring the looks of pity, and the occasional moisture in her eyes that this would be her last day at work before the dreaded curse was to take place. Everyone had been on best behavior today, bringing in flowers and treats to their beloved boss on what was assumed to be her last day of wakeful life.

Rory ignored the sadness and looked over the sketches. "This one," she said with a firm nod. "Can I see the options for the benefit next month?"

"Of course, Lady Aurora."

Rory kept her mind on her tasks, but stiffened when she heard a voice she'd know anywhere shouting her name.

"Rory, my love! Happy early birthday!"

Rory paled when none other than Prince Henry himself rounded the corner. He knew how to behave like the royal he was, but every now and then the pressure to perform perfectly for the public grew too excruciating, so he let his true personality fly high. "Henry? What are you doing here?" she asked quietly through terse lips. She loathed being the center of attention in a crowd, and Henry knew just how to make her squirm. Everyone had turned in their chairs, some rising while others knelt in respect to the throne.

All eyes drew to the six-foot-two handsome blond prince with the rakish grin. His voice was loud, which was nothing unusual. But untethered like this, he seemed louder, his hand gestures bigger, and his smile even more dashing. He clutched a bouquet of a dozen red roses in his fist, and his matching designer scarf wafted out behind him as he beelined for his mark.

Remus heard the commotion and opened his office door that was beside Rory's, smirking at the man he'd known since birth.

"Remus, old friend!"

Remus expected Henry to throw his arms around him, as he always did, but Henry was especially rascally, since he was prowling the area with only his personal guard, who stood stoically at the entrance like a gargoyle. Instead of a hug, Henry yanked Remus by the tie and laid a quick peck to his lips, laughing at the shock on Remus' face when he released the man.

A few nearby workers squeaked at the scene of their elusive in-control vice president looking so very ruffled. A few clapped at the show, and the buzz picked up as the eyes that were always hungry for gossip zeroed in on the newcomer. A few phones found their way out of pockets and purses, snapping shots of the prince invading their workspace for the sheer purpose of pleasure.

Remus wiped off his mouth, red-faced and looking as if he'd eaten something sour. "Henry, you can't just come in here and..."

"And sweep my future bride off her feet? Darling!" Henry threw his arms wide, grinning at the chaos he was creating. His life was so controlled back in the palace. To let himself loose breathed new life into his naturally playful disposition.

Cordray was a statue as Rory turned red, stammering for Henry to knock it off. "Henry, you know that's not..."

But Rory never finished her sentence. Henry smacked the roses down on her assistant's desk, climbed overtop of it in true dramatic fashion, and leaped onto her side of the divide. He scooped Rory's face in his palms and laid a kiss on her so grand, that every woman in the office swooned. He wrapped his arms around her, pulling back so his voice could carry as if he was addressing the entire office, who were gathering around to gawk with delight. "Today! Today, my love. I cannot wait another moment for our wedding. Let's elope, and then spend your birthday making lots of babies. I know the exact angle I'll need to use to make us a boy. That silly curse won't last a minute if I'm around to vanquish it!"

Rory was positively crimson, and wished to run away. Of course, Henry knew this about her, so he held her tighter, smiling at her squirm. "Henry, you're being ridiculous." Then she lowered her voice to a whisper. "You know I'm seeing someone."

Henry kissed her again, and then tipped his head back with a mournful cry. "Cut me to the quick, woman! Who? Who shall I joust to win back your favor?"

"Let go of her," came a low growl to Rory's left. Cordray's fists were clenched at his sides, the only angry person in the sea of enthralled gawkers. "I won't ask you a second time."

"You! And what claim do you have on my love's heart?" Then his eyebrows pulled together. "Hey, I know you."

Henry released Rory, who stepped back and tried to appeal to Cord.

"I'm her boyfriend!" Cordray roared, his temper finally hitting its breaking point. His fist flew without warning, without hesitation, and without apology, cracking across Henry's square jaw.

The prince let out a bleat of pain, and then cried out with hysterical laughter. "That was incredible! What a swing! And the joust begins!"

Henry's guard wasn't so forgiving. In the next second, Cordray found himself with his torso lying flat across Francesca's desk, the agenda for the day smashed to his cheek as the formidable Victor held him down.

Remus ran to the desk, swearing as he explained in hushed tones to Henry's guard that Cordray was no threat to the throne. Benjamin burst through the front door, adding to the torrents of gasps and freshly-milled gossip when he assessed the situation as quickly as he could, and swept Rory off her feet in true bodyguard fashion. He ran her out the backdoor, despite her protests that it was all a big misunderstanding.

21

CORDRAY AND HENRY

"Put me down, Benjamin!" Rory insisted, kicking her legs until he consented at the end of the alley.

"I'm parked over there. Go!"

Rory remained firm. "No, you don't understand. Henry was pulling his usual 'I'm going to marry Rory' practical joke, and Cord punched him. Then Victor got involved, and Remus is left to deal with it all. I have to go back in there!"

"You're not in danger?"

"No, Henry's in danger from me! I'm going to wring that boy's neck!" She stomped back toward the entrance, but it flew open seconds before her fingers could close on the handle.

Henry and Cordray were both being held by their collars, and were shoved out into the alley by Remus and

Victor, who frowned at them both. The men spilled out into the cold, shoving each other with very different expressions. Cordray looked positively murderous, but Henry was a puppy who wasn't cunning enough to understand the difference between being bopped on the nose with a newspaper, and when someone was playing fetch with him.

Remus shoved Cordray to the end of the alley near Benjamin, and Victor pushed Henry in the opposite direction. Remus rubbed out a crease on his forehead. "Are you quite satisfied with the chaos, Henry? Honestly. Now I have to go in there and explain that away somehow."

"Explain what away? Get the gossip mill churning. Give the people a good scandal to focus on, rather than Malaura's curse."

"Oh, you're impossible." Rory blanched, and then pulled a wad of blue gum from her mouth. "I think this belongs to you. So gross, Henry."

Cordray was far from calmed. He lunged at Henry again, landing a shot to his kidney that brought the prince to his knees. Benjamin wrestled Cord off of the prince, and Victor helped his charge to his feet.

The two guards locked eyes, each taking an opposite end of the alley to watch while the others sorted out the mess that Henry was so proud of stirring up.

Rory hugged herself to stave off the frosty weather. She wore a gray skirt and a black camisole under a gray blouse that had ruffles along the hem, which was slightly less warm than a proper jacket. "Can you give us a minute to sort this out?"

"Please." Remus ran his hand over his face. "And Henry? Warn me the next time you kiss me. I'll be sure to suck on a moldy old sock in anticipation."

"Best kiss of your life," Henry replied, waggling his eyebrows as he rose to his feet.

Remus went back into the building, shaking his head, and leaving the trio to duke it out in the alley.

Cordray glared at Rory, jabbing his finger toward Henry, who was still grinning. "This guy? This is how your best friend behaves around you?"

"Henry's harmless," Rory assured him, ignoring Henry's guffaw. "He does that sometimes – stirs up trouble because he's bored cooped up in the palace, or to steer the public's focus away from other, more harrowing things. Though, a warning would have been nice." She glared at her friend.

Henry's eyes danced with playfulness that never seemed to dull. "Where's the fun in warning you? I was hoping you'd slap me, so the people will be all a dither, wondering if we're in love, and if I can break the curse or not."

She palmed Henry's churlish grin so she didn't have to look at it anymore. "He doesn't mean anything by it. We've never been together. Honest."

Henry postured. "I'll have you know that I'm not harmless. I'm deviously plotting my way into my darling Rory's heart. I'm taking the long con, spending twenty-four long years trying to woo her."

Rory rolled her eyes and shoved him lightly backward. "Like anyone's going to believe that. Cord, nothing's going on. I'm with you. Only you."

Cordray kept his finger leveled in Henry's face. "I trust her, but I don't want you sniffing around my girlfriend if I'm not there to keep you from humping her leg. She's not up for grabs, so you'll back off, now that you've had your fun. You sent your message to the people, and now it's over."

Henry grabbed his chest as if his heart was mid-rupture. "Rory, tell this brute how many times you've seen me naked."

"Zero!" Rory blushed. "Oh my gosh, do you have an off switch? Victor, can you put a muzzle on your village idiot?"

Victor's mouth twitched, but he didn't reply. He'd been with the royal family since Rory was a child, and barely spoke to anyone.

Rory moved into Cordray's body space, shivering as she held his face to get him to focus on only her. "Cord, it's only you. There's no one else. Please believe me."

"I think I do." His face was stern as he looked down into her pleading eyes. "But I don't want other men kissing you."

"Only you," she assured him. "I've never had a

boyfriend before, so Henry hasn't had a chance to adjust to the new dynamic. Please, Cord."

Cordray held onto his anger for another handful of seconds, and then the tension in his shoulders began to loosen. "Tell me again."

"Only you," she cooed, lifting herself up onto her toes and kissing him in plain view of Henry. She ran her fingertips up the hard planes of his chest, holding onto his collar as she kissed him again, her frozen breath tickling his nose. "It was you from the first day we met."

Henry cleared his throat three times before they broke it up. He took in Cordray's scowl with a hearty grin. "I take it we're adding a fourth to the elite three, then?"

Rory turned in Cordray's arms, nodding. "Yes, and the two of you will get along with Cord. Do you understand?"

"Now that I know exactly how Cord likes to be kissed, I'd be happy to add him into my rotation. It's just as well. Remus was an absolute chore to kiss. One might assume he didn't want to be doing it at all." Henry winked at Cordray, whose nostrils flared.

Since the tension had been slightly lessened, Rory finally broke into a smile. "You're here. I can't believe you're here."

Henry's smile turned from caddish to sincere at her wonder. "Of course I am. Did you really think I'd leave you with only one guard so near to your twenty-fifth birthday? Proposals and roses aside, I love you. What's more, I know you. I know you're more worried than you let on. So I thought I'd come with an extra guard for your safety, plus a whole load of distractions to keep you from driving yourself into a nervous frenzy."

Rory's hand pressed over her chest, touched at the thoughtfulness. "Really? You didn't have to do all that. I'm really fine. Just a little anxious, is all."

Henry pulled her into his arms, pressing his cheek to the top of her head. He had a charming way about him that made people consider foolish choices they might not otherwise indulge in. "That's why I'm here. I thought I'd lend my muscle, plus Victor's, to curb your dreaded curse. Tonight, we celebrate. It's your last weekend being twenty-four, and you're here working? That sounds like a wasted opportunity. Leave early and be irresponsible with me. Cord, too. I think it's time we broke him in, if you're serious about the man. I had no idea. When you told me you were seeing someone, I only thought you were trying to make me jealous and break my fragile heart."

Rory sniggered at the joke. "Poor brokenhearted Prince Henry."

"Indeed. This is the one, though? The man you fancy?"

Rory squeezed Cordray's hand. "It is."

"Excellent. Then he'll come along. I've got it all planned out. First, we go snowmobiling, then we go out for a lavish meal, in which I'll propose to you all over again. I'm thinking this time, you should say no, and smack me across the face. Be all haughty and superior, so I can garner the pity of any females nearby."

Cordray frowned. "How often do you ask Rory to marry you?"

Henry shrugged. "However often it occurs to me – whenever I'm bored, or the world needs a distraction." Then he pretended to do a doubletake and clutched his chest as if enraptured anew by Rory's beauty. "My love, throw this brute aside, come away to my palace and marry me!" he crooned, getting down on one knee.

Rory chuckled, now that Cordray was seeing the full breadth of Henry's personality and managed not to get riled up at the game. "Not today. I've got a date with my boyfriend and my bestie."

"Two besties, actually," Henry corrected her with a secretive smirk. "Right this way, milady." He popped his elbow out to her, but Cordray drew her to his other side, putting himself in the middle. "Touché," Henry said under his breath, sizing Cord up appreciatively. Henry led the way past Victor and out into the parking lot, where a town car waited for them.

He opened the backdoor for Rory, who gasped. "Adam! You came out of your castle for me?"

Adam shot her a surly look and didn't make a move to get out and greet her. He kept to the opposite side to avoid any errant glances that might fall his way. His collar was turned up to shield him further, with a scarf covering the lower part of his face. His voice was surly and embarrassed that somehow Henry had coaxed him to participate in the levity. "Don't make a big deal of it. I'm here. Happy birthday. You can pick your present from this catalog, and no, I'm not wrapping it. Get in and choose something sparkly. I couldn't care less what it is."

Rory looked up at Cordray, who shrugged. "I haven't been snowmobiling since college."

Rory beamed up at him, grateful he was willing to give her oddball friends a try. "Don't worry. I'll be gentle."

22

BIRTHDAY EVE

The snow fell heavy outside the mansion as Rory clutched her cup of hot cocoa. Echoes of the laughter from the evening of pre-birthday fun were beginning to die as the night set in, and her parents retired to their bedroom. Cordray had been almost as much of a daredevil as Henry, and the two egged each other on to jump bigger hills and go faster around dodgy turns. Adam had remained by her side, riding at a brisk but reasonable pace through the woods near Henry's cabin. Though Adam was around the same age as Henry, he'd always seemed much, much older to Rory.

Of course, Benjamin hadn't permitted her to ride by herself. He'd held onto her waist as she controlled the pace and daring of her snowmobile.

The house was quiet, but for the thrumming of her heart as she waited until she was certain her parents and the staff were asleep. She hadn't changed into her pajamas, but wore her usual business clothes – black slacks, a gray top and a charcoal cardigan.

Her mind drifted to worry as the minutes ticked by, inching closer and closer to the dreaded day the curse was coming due. She talked a good game that she wasn't worried about Malaura's curse, but as she waited standing in the window of her bedroom, her palms began to sweat. There was so much she hadn't experienced, even though she'd tried to cram as much life experience and accomplishments into her twenty-five years. Though, looking back on her life now, she wondered if she'd put a few things off because they were too risky, too public, or required her to ask for use of Remus' magic, which she refused to do. He'd sacrificed too much for her already.

Rory swallowed hard and took a chance, setting her mug down and calling Adam, even though they'd just spent the evening together.

"What?" came his signature growl. It didn't matter if she called him at ten in the morning or midnight, he was surly at all hours. That he answered his phone for her was a grand tribute to their friendship; he wouldn't offer another kindness on top of that.

She fiddled with the hem of her gray v-neck, the soft cotton sliding between her fingers as she picked at a stray thread. "Tell me my curse isn't anything to worry about."

Adam didn't answer at first, but rather breathed into the phone for several beats. Rory knew Adam understood the gravity of curses; he'd been deformed by one easily enough. He had just over a year before the last petal was predicted to fall from the enchanted rose Malaura had given him when she'd cursed him. After that, he was doomed to join the Lupine – a group of cursed men and women who had befallen similar fates, unable to escape Malaura's wrath. The pack of wolves were outcasts from society and had lost everything upon their transition. The Lupine couldn't vote, couldn't own property, and weren't thought of as people any longer once they went through the change from human to enormous wolf.

When Adam finally spoke, Rory felt her knees start to weaken. "You know I can't tell you that."

She gripped the windowsill to keep herself from teetering, and then nodded with her eyes closed. "If I prick my finger tomorrow, and Remus' counter-curse actually works, will you..." She wished he would fill in the gaps, so she didn't have to say the embarrassing words, but Adam remained silent, never speaking unless absolutely necessary. She'd already had this talk with Henry, who'd assured her without a doubt that it was already in his plan to try and wake her, if it was in his power to do so. She swallowed hard, summoning up her gumption and gulping back her insecurities. "If Cord and Henry can't wake me, will you try?" Pressure began to build up behind her eyes, making everything feel that much more humiliating as she waited for his response.

Adam sighed heavily. "You know that won't work. We're not in love."

A solitary tear spilled down her cheek, marring the creamy skin with a tract of desperation. "But if we were, Remus' counter-curse would work, and I'd wake right back up! I'm not asking you for anything but a chance. Please. If they can't wake me, I need to know you'll try. I'm barely holding it together here."

Adam's snarl could be heard clearly, and Rory could picture his furry upper lip curling with distaste. "We had a great evening, and here you go, getting all emotional."

"Please, Adam! If there was a chance I could undo your curse, I would try anything!"

"Fine!" he roared, making Rory shake under the weight of his rage. "If Henry and Cord can't wake you, I'll give it a try. Make sure there's a photographer there, though. Wouldn't want to miss out on getting a picture of the grand moment. I can see the headlines now: The Beast Scares Sleeping Beauty out of her Coma."

Rory wanted to snap at his temper, but she knew there was no point. Adam had grown bitter and mean, and no amount of any sort of pleading would soften him. She'd accomplished what she wanted, so she decided not to push him any further. "Thank you," she said, and then hung up before Adam could say anything that might bait her to bite back.

It took a solid five minutes to rid herself of her tears, but finally, she was able to appreciate her view of the moon for what it was – a solitary light in the sky that shone brightly, regardless of how kind the stars were to her.

When the clock struck eleven, Rory finished her beverage and slid her winter coat back on, knowing exactly whose arms she wanted to be in when she closed her eyes. She held her shoes and padded in her socks down the hallway, not turning on any lights as she felt her way toward the side door on the main floor. She tiptoed through the kitchen, but nearly shrieked when the lights flipped on, illuminating her escape. "Benjamin! What are you doing? You nearly gave me a heart attack."

Benjamin was standing by the side door, leaning against the wall with too much understanding in his gaze. "You pack quite well for a sleepwalker."

She met his eyes with a defiance she rarely bothered him with. She ran through a list of excuses, but the winter jacket and shoes were pretty damning. Instead of fighting it, she rolled her shoulders back and raised her chin. "I'm going out, and you'll let me."

Benjamin shrugged. "Since when have I ever barricaded you in the house? Go wherever you like. This isn't the palace. You're a grown woman. By all means, sneak away."

Rory froze, not wanting to question the too-good-to-be-true offer. "Okay," she replied slowly, and inched for the door he was standing next to.

"Of course, I'll be driving you to wherever it is you

haven't told anyone you're going. Meeting Cord somewhere?"

Rory's shoulders slumped. "Please, Benjamin. I never ask you for anything. Just think, you could've gotten stuck guarding Henry, or any number of dignitaries who could've made your job a nightmare. Give me this one night, Benjamin. Please."

Benjamin met her gaze with his own brand of scrutiny that had seen through many a nefarious character. He reached out and wrapped her in a hug they rarely exchanged, but never denied each other. "I held you the day you were born, you know. I was only twenty, and fresh out of the Academy. Your father wanted someone more experienced, but your mother saw something in me. She told me I could work for the family as long as I took care of you, so that's what I did. Your first step. Every first day of school. Every birthday. Every test day. Every workday. Every weekend. All of it, I've been there. But now you're asking me to let you go? This close to the finish line?" He squeezed her and shook his head. "For the next twenty-four hours, you and I don't separate. We'll eat together, sleep in the same room, all of it. You can sneak out to wherever you like, but I'm sneaking with you. That's the best offer you'll get, kiddo."

Rory slumped in his arms. "You won't approve, but it has to be done."

"Talk to me."

"No."

It was gentle, the Pulse that Benjamin began to thrum into her. She was sensitive enough to his nuances that she could pick up the subconscious suggestion easily enough. "Tell me why you're sneaking around tonight. Tell me where we're going."

Rory gritted her teeth, but Benjamin's Pulse was well-honed from years of interrogating her family's attackers. Benjamin's self-loathing was visible as he Pulsed the truth from her. He could feel the trust crumbling on both ends of their friendship that had taken decades to build.

Rory debated trying to shove him and fight her way out, but she didn't have the heart to raise her hand to Benjamin. "Please, Benji." She invoked the nickname she'd used for him when she was a little girl, and had been too young to attempt three-syllable words. "I wanted to go to Cord's condo. When I prick my finger, I want to fall asleep in his arms, so I can wake right back up. I don't want to go out like this, barely having cracked the surface of all I want to accomplish in life! I don't want to waste away in a sterile bed somewhere." Her voice climbed to a hysterical pitch as she pictured her body laid out in a shapeless gown, tubes running in and out of her. "Don't let me rot away in a hospital!"

He shushed her, his cheek pressed to the top of her head. "It's okay. I won't let you rot. I'll be with you every second of every day until you wake back up. You think you're tired of me now? Wait until your coma. You won't be able to push me away then. I'll read you my Westerns that you hate, and sing so off-key that you'll wake just to shut me up."

Despite the seriousness of the moment, Rory softened in her guard's arms. "Tell me I'm worrying over nothing."

"Why you ever worry about anything at all when I'm around is beyond me." He pressed a chaste kiss to her temple. "Let's go."

Rory's eyes widened. "Really?"

Benjamin's mouth pulled to the side. "Did you honestly think I'd let you hole up here? It's the first place Malaura will come looking. It's all been arranged."

Leah and Stefan came down the stairs, each with a suitcase in their hands. "Three cars going three separate directions. I'll make sure I'm seen far away from you," Leah promised. "That might draw them out my way."

Stefan kissed his daughter's forehead and clapped Benjamin on the back. "I'll do the same."

Rory's head whipped from Benjamin to her parents, shocked that this had all been planned without her. "Wait, no! We should stay together."

Leah had tears glistening in her eyes. "And this is how we'll make that happen. Separate for one day, and then we'll get to keep each other forever. This will work, honey. Go with Benjamin. Your safehouse is already set up."

"Where? Mom, I don't like this."

Stefan smiled at his daughter, and Rory could see the softness in his eyes he often got when he was remembering what she looked like as a baby. "I ordered a birthday cake for you. It's waiting at your safehouse, but we'll celebrate properly next week, when all of this madness is behind us."

Panic welled in Rory's throat, but she swallowed it down, knowing that if something bad was coming for her, she wanted it far away from her family. At least this way they would be safe. Moisture pressed behind her eyes, and nearly spilled over when her mother caught her in a tight hug, and then handed her over to her father for an embrace that squeezed a few tears from her. "Daddy?" she whispered.

Stefan held Rory tighter, and it wasn't until Benjamin cleared his throat that he released his daughter into the arms of the man who'd been trusted with her safety since her birth. He cupped Benjamin's shoulder and squeezed. "Tell me again that this is the right move."

"This is the only move," he assured the Chancellor. "I'll return her in twenty-four hours."

It wasn't her father's forced expression of bravery, but her mother's growing sobs she tried to muffle in her hand that made Rory's knees start to tremble. Anxiety over parting from her parents gripped her around the throat, choking any profound parting words she wanted to utter.

Then they were gone, and Rory felt the hard swing of fear threaten to take her to a place she wouldn't return from. She couldn't give a voice to her terror if she wanted to make it through the next day.

Trepidation filled Rory like sand, slowing her movements as she plodded into the garage through the side door and ducked into the back, seeing an overnight bag already packed and ready to go. She jumped when the backdoor opened, and her uncle slid in beside her. "Uncle Remus! What are you doing here?"

He shot her a withering look, his gray slacks and light green dress shirt never daring to wrinkle. "Did you honestly think I have it in me to leave your protection to anyone else? You sincerely underestimate my controlling nature if you think I'm taking a breather now."

She reached over and squeezed his hand, gratitude welling up inside of her. "Thank you."

"There's nothing to worry about. I'm here."

When the driver's door opened, her hands found her way back to her lap, and she began twisting the fabric of her shirt nervously. If Remus was concerned enough not to let her go through this last stretch without him, then she knew there was very real reason to be afraid. "Benjamin?" she croaked, her voice and her bravery forsaking her.

Benjamin started up the car after two more guards slid in, giving Rory slight nods of assurance. Though she knew them well enough as palace guards on loan from King Hubert, she reached over and clutched Remus' hand as she'd done when she was a child and needed to steady herself for the press. The simple touch held her to the planet as the garage door creaked open, and the cavalcade of black cars rolled slowly out into the night.

23

THE SAFEHOUSE

Rory was quiet during the hour-long drive out of the main city. When the clock ticked past midnight, the guards were on high alert. The one on her right slanted his body sideways to shield her, even though no one could see past the tinted windows, much less in the dark. No one spoke, not even when the buildings gave way to thick knots of trees that told her the safehouse would be well off the beaten path.

When her phone rang, Remus checked the caller ID before handing Rory her phone. "Hello?" she said quietly.

"I'm shocked, utterly shocked that you're not peacefully sleeping right now."

Rory managed a small indulgent smile. "Good evening, Papa Hubert. I'm surprised you're awake."

"Do you know how proud I am of you?"

Tears welled in her eyes that bore no shame. She

wanted to respond, but all speech felt stuck in her throat like too much peanut butter.

"You saw the burden the government was bearing, financing the entire educational system, and you understood we weren't capable of providing the best for our people. You saw that we were focusing too much on magical training, and not enough on reading, writing and arithmetic. So you took it upon yourself to start your Foundation, making sure everyone had access to free, comprehensive traditional schooling, regardless of their income or social status."

When she finally found her voice, it was small and childlike. She pictured King Hubert's face as she remembered it from her childhood, when her, Adam and Henry begged him for scary stories before bedtime. "It's no trouble. I'm happy to serve Avondale however it needs me."

"Do you know that I love you as if you were my own daughter?"

Her chest warmed as Remus squeezed her free hand, as if to echo the king's words. "I love you, too, Papa."

The king cleared his throat. "Very good. Now that that's out of the way, I expect you'll come by the palace after you're finished with this gratuitous nap you're bent on indulging in." He pretended to scold her, making her laugh airily through her nose. Then his voice grew somber. "If you're anxious at all, call me. I'll make sure my phone is on me at all hours. Unfortunately, the guards I pay far too much are forcing Henry and I to stay in the palace for the next twenty-four hours, otherwise I would be by your side. Promise me you'll call often."

"I will. Thank you, Papa."

"I love you, dear. Sleep well."

Rory blinked away her tears, taking a few steadying breaths. "I should call Cord when we get there to let him know where I'm at."

Remus kept his eyes on their surroundings. "You can do that once we get there."

Rory ached to have this day over with, but knew the longest day of her life was only beginning. When Benjamin pulled down an unpaved road an hour later, portions of the scenery were beginning to look familiar to her. "Benjamin? Where did you say we were going?"

"Somewhere no one will look for you. The owner of the house was only too happy to give it to us for your birthday."

Rory's spirits picked up when they pulled in behind the cabin she knew quite well. There were men in black suits dotting the property, each giving a nod to the town car and waving it forward. "This was your plan?" she squeaked, overjoyed at the fortunate turn of events.

Benjamin smirked at her in the rearview mirror. "Happy birthday, kiddo. Let the guys check the grounds first, and then we can go on in."

Rory was practically bouncing in her seat as she waited, a giddy grin on her face. In all her imaginings of this day, she never thought she would be smiling, nor did she envision herself at the cabin that had started her off down the road to optimism. She hadn't entertained such hope for a remedy to her curse until she'd met the only man who'd so thoroughly captured her heart.

When the palace guards escorted her from the car to the cabin, Rory ran into her boyfriend's arms, a gust of relief shaking a few tears loose. "You didn't tell me this was the plan!"

"What's the point of a birthday surprise if you already know what it is? Did you have any trouble on your way in?"

Rory shook her head, and then buried her nose in Cordray's shoulder, inhaling his freshly-showered scent as if it was the only thing that gave her lungs permission to breathe. "You're the best birthday gift ever. Thank you for this."

"Happy birthday, Story. I know it's late, but I was thinking you might want to open one of your presents before you tuck on in for the night."

"Oh, I couldn't sleep if my life depended on it." Her fingers flitted along his swollen forearm. "You got me a present?"

"Presents, but you only get one for now."

Rory leaned up and kissed him, despite the stony-faced guards that were mulling around in the cabin. The two laced their fingers together, reveling in the sensation of holding hands without gloves. The second pill had done the trick, taking away his magic so he couldn't harm her with an errant touch.

They were all smiles as Cord led the way to his bedroom upstairs, waggling his eyebrows suggestively as he opened the door. "This isn't exactly how I pictured a weekend with you back at my cabin, but I'll take what I can get."

"What could be more romantic than you, me, and a dozen or so palace guards?"

Cordray popped open his bedroom door and took a step inside with a grand sweeping gesture, revealing a pillow on the bed with a red satin bow tied around it. When Rory didn't say anything, Cordray coiled his arm around her hips and pulled her to his chest. "It's yours for when you sleep over. I was thinking after this curse business is done with, we could spend weekends up here, away from it all. It could be *our* cabin, instead of just mine."

Rory had been too anxious to be expecting birthday presents, much less one that held so much meaning. Tenderness softened her gaze as she parted from him to run her hand over the simple gift that made her heart sing with all the emotion of a finely tuned violin. She sat on the edge of his bed and pulled the pillow onto her lap, fiddling with the lacy case as she hugged the treasure. Her voice was small but steady as she met his gaze across the way. "If I could have only one wish, it would be for more time with you."

Cordray smirked at her sincerity. "Aw, don't waste a

wish on that. If you only had one? You should wish for a mattress here that's slightly less lumpy."

"I'm the birthday girl, and you're my wish."

When he moseyed toward her, she fisted the fabric of his shirt and pulled him down for a kiss, leaning backward onto the mattress to make the most of their few minutes alone. His lips were soft and insistent as he climbed atop her, giving them both taste after taste of something precious to hold onto while they waited out the storm together.

The voice that interrupted them from the doorway made Cordray jump off of her. "Raven's secure. I'll keep eyes on her."

Rory deflated and sat up, offering a wan smile at the guard. "Hey, Luke. Did you get a new suit?"

Luke offered a small snort to her jab at the standard black suit that never changed. "Dressed up for the birthday girl."

Cordray shot the guard a withering look and turned back to Rory. "So much for that. You want to go back downstairs?"

"Nah. This is the most privacy we'll be getting."

The two settled on watching a movie in bed. Though they were fully clothed with shoes on in case they needed to bolt at a moment's notice, they still got under the covers, snuggling close as they both pretended that the world outside didn't mean to tear them apart. Rory tucked herself in Cordray's arm, letting herself believe in the safety his solid form provided.

Neither of them really watched the movie, nor did Luke, who stood at the bedroom window, peeking through the corner of the closed curtain for any signs of Malaura making her move. The television was kept at a low volume, so as not to disturb the silence that felt utterly suffocating.

It was slow at first – her breathing slightly more labored than it had been moments before. She blamed it on the late hour, and the fact that she was trying to stay up all night during a fairly stressful time. She cuddled into Cordray, but found him already asleep.

It wasn't until ten seconds later, when Luke's eyes rolled back and he batted at the air in an attempt to stay upright that Rory realized something was very wrong. Luke fell to his knees, and Rory muffled her scream into her pillow as she found just enough strength to sit up. She breathed into the lace, unsure what was going on that made exhaustion sweep over them all so deftly. Reaching for her phone, she called the one number she knew would never fail her. "Uncle Remus?" she worked out, her lungs laboring under the effort.

"Something's off. I can feel it." His tone was tinged with a darkened edge. "I can feel *her*. Are you okay?"

"Gas leak!" Then her fingers started to lose all feeling, and her phone slipped from her grip.

She cried out when an explosion from outside lit up

the night, flickering across the curtains with a fire that began to crackle on the branches.

Then two more blasts shook the house and rattled her bones. Terror raked through her nerves when she realized Cordray wasn't moving, and Luke was still motionless on the floor. She knew she didn't have much time as she slid off the bed to fumble with her phone on the floor. Remus was no longer on the other end, so she called the police, breathing slowly into the phone. "This is Aurora Johnstone. Malaura found me."

It was all she could work out before her hand lost its commitment to holding the device. Hopelessness rattled inside her chest as her phone clattered to the floor in time with the front door downstairs opening on creaky hinges.

The footsteps didn't hurry, but tapped out the rhythm to Rory's sluggish heartbeat.

"Happy birthday, Aurora," came a voice she'd hoped she would never hear again.

The sound of Malaura sent fresh terror down her spine. She gasped, which only forced more of the polluted air down her esophagus. Her vision swam, but she saw the superior glint to the stony eyes that had once ruled Avondale without compassion for its people. The evil queen moved into the bedroom with a man in a black ski mask by her side, a fog emanating out from his palms. Rory tried to get up and fight with the last vestiges of her energy, but she could scarcely do more than sit on her own. Her heart stuttered in her chest. All the trouble of trying to avoid fate, but it had found her anyway, stalking her in the dead of night into the woods.

Malaura gripped Rory's face with one hand, a sneer tugging at her red painted lips. "I could kill you right now, I hope you know. But I won't, because I'm a merciful queen. I think I'll let my Remus find you deep in your sleep, so he can see exactly how unworthy he was of my attention. He turned his back on me to watch over you. How foolish. I could've given him the world, but he chose to fret over a Deadpulse." She shook her head, tsking Rory. "I'll never understand the burden of familial ties."

"Remus!" Rory tried to work out, but her voice could barely be heard as it escaped her lips.

"I've found a new prize student now, and he'll do nicely. I've had eyes on you for quite some time, Aurora. I guess I should thank you for leading me to someone worthy of my focus." Her eyes climbed to Cordray, who was knocked out, helpless atop the mattress.

"No!" Rory tried to shout, but the sound came out mumbled and weak. Her lashes fluttered shut, and she knew that if her uncle hadn't yet thundered up the steps to stop his former tutor, that he was most certainly down for the count.

Knocked out, she told herself firmly. *She could never kill him.*

There was a prick on Rory's finger, and suddenly, she felt like she was floating. She'd always assumed she would get to see the weapon that took her down, but the fog taking over her vision clouded out the deadly details. Suddenly there was no more arduous worry to her breathing, only stillness. Weightlessness.

"Sleep well, Aurora. We'll see how the kingdom that abandoned me fares now."

24

ELECTRIC

"**C**ome on, now. Wake up. We didn't hit you that hard."

Cordray felt a hand slap against his cheek three times, his face sticky with saliva and something viscous. His eyelids felt heavy, but eventually, he coaxed them to open. The world spun in sickening shades of gray, green and black, so he closed his eyes again until he was certain he wouldn't vomit if the room spun again.

"There you go. Awake, finally. You've got to develop a thicker skin if you're going to keep up. You can't go all soft like a baby the first time you're hit."

Cordray frowned, his lips puffy. His mouth felt dry, and his teeth had a ringing sensation to them that he couldn't remedy even after opening his mouth wide to stretch his jaw. "Where am I?"

"You're home, brother. We're the people you belong

with, Cordray." The man had a few missing teeth, but looked friendly enough. He had a burn mark on his left cheek, but a brightness to his gray eyes that gave Cord something to focus on. "I'm Dustin, one of the people who rescued you."

"Rescued me?" Cordray asked as he cracked his sore neck. He took Dustin's gloved hand and brought himself up to sitting – though that took more effort than he'd been anticipating.

"We're the Queen's Lethals," Dustin proclaimed with pride, puffing out his chest. He wore an unwashed blue mechanic's shirt that was missing a button at the pooched waist. "Shame that you hide your gifts. The world doesn't appreciate us."

Cord tried to hold onto Dustin's words and sift them into the proper order in his groggy mind. "Wait, how do you know my name?"

"Everything about you is in your file."

"My file?" Cordray rubbed his forehead. "Where am I?" He blinked again, and the room became clearer. The concrete walls matched the cold floor, and both were covered in cobwebs and something that looked like a putrid green fungus. He shivered and looked down to see his shirt torn at the shoulder, smeared with dirt and grime.

"You're home. We take care of our own, especially since no one's going to look after us."

"We?"

"Lethals. You're Electric. I wanted your name to be

Zapper. Then people could call you the Mad Zapper, but 'Electric' was the one that stuck. Sorry, man."

Cordray smacked his lips, grimacing at the funny flavor in his mouth. "How am I here?"

"We've got eyes on the Chancellor and his daughter. Make sure everything goes according to the queen's plan. We've known about you for weeks."

Cord's eyes widened. "It was one of you who attacked Rory in the restaurant."

"Of course. We didn't care about taking her down then. It was to see if you would react."

Cordray stretched his back, which felt like it was in desperate need of a chiropractor. "You should be arrested."

"We're not criminals," Dustin retorted with his chin raised petulantly.

"Of course not. You only attacked the Chancellor's daughter after breaking into my house. Then you abducted me. What's wrong with that?" He frowned at Dustin, who he guessed he was slightly bigger than. Though, his body felt like it had just been put through an industrial clothing dryer, so it was anybody's guess who would win in a fistfight. "If you wanted a conversation with me to explain your politics in all of it, you could've just talked to me, you know."

Dustin shook his head, his arms crossed over his chest. "Not with Aurora around. She knows most of our faces. Besides, we had to get you away from them first. Otherwise they could keep poisoning your mind with their self-righteous filth."

"Rory isn't self-righteous," Cordray grumbled, taking his time as he stood to his feet. He stretched out his back and heard several unsettling pops and cracks that made him feel like an old man.

"Maybe not outright, but her parents are. And Remus, of course. But Aurora's nothing to us. She kept Remus distracted well enough while we assembled and gathered more of our kind."

Cord clenched his hands into fists. "I've got to get back." Cordray knew it wouldn't be that simple, but he had to try.

Dustin stood from his stool and blocked the doorway in the empty room. "You're staying with us. The Chancellor will have his hands full for a long time. He won't even notice you're gone."

"I was taken right out of my house! Of course they'll come looking for me."

Dustin shrugged, and then delivered his hard truth to the newcomer. "You're a Lethal. You don't matter to them one bit." He wore a saddened expression, as if he pitied Cord for not understanding the harsh ways of the world. "How many of us have gone missing in the past year, only to end up with a piss-poor police job in the hunts to find us? All because we're inconvenient to society."

Cordray knew Dustin was needling him, but the panic

started to eat at his insides all the same. "You're wrong. I don't want to hurt you, man. Let me out, and we're cool."

Dustin cracked his knuckles and held up his hands as if he was readying to catch a baseball. "You're welcome to try it, brother, but I wish you wouldn't."

Cordray didn't feel completely ready for a fistfight, but he came out swinging all the same. Though the pill was muting his electric current, it did nothing to hamper his strength that had been earned the old-fashioned way – chopping wood in the forest. He was proud of his aim that rang true when he socked Dustin across the face.

It wasn't Dustin who cried out, though. With a simple touch, Cordray found all the air sucked from his lungs. He fell to his knees, gasping and holding his throat as he struggled for air.

Dustin crouched in front of him, a sympathetic look on his face as he clapped Cordray on the back. "You really don't know much about your own people, do you. I'm a Suffocant. The papers call me Sycophant the Suffocant. See, that's why I wanted to get you a good nickname. You get a stupid one, and it follows you around forever. What you're feeling now is me taking all the air from your lungs. If I concentrate with all my might and squeeze too hard, I can collapse your lung, but see, I don't want to do that. We're not all the monsters the Chancellor thinks we are. You took a swing at me, so I'm defending myself with the weapon nature gave me." He shook his head in dismay as Cordray's eyes began to bug out in distress. "And to think, there are people out there who want to leave me defenseless. The Chancellor's daughter is a Deadpulse, so he wants to make all of us useless. That pill you took? It'll make you just like a Deadpulse for an entire month. That's not something any of us should have to tolerate." He pushed out a chuckle and slapped Cordray on the back, forcing a flood of oxygen back into his lungs. "But see? All it takes is a little self-control. Same as people who go off and buy guns. No harm, no foul. I've never killed anyone who didn't deserve it."

A heavy set of boots tromped down the hallway, and when the door swung open, a man in all black stared down at the two with a bland expression on his face. "The queen wants to meet Electric."

Dustin rolled his eyes at the nickname that was far from his first choice. "Alright, Jared. He's coming."

Without waiting for the prisoner to catch his breath, Jared and Dustin hoisted Cordray to his feet, leading him along as Cord stumbled down the dimly lit hallway toward his doom.

25

QUEEN OF THE DEAD

Cordray wasn't sure what he expected Malaura to be like. The last photo he'd seen of her was nearly a decade old. Part of him wondered if she wasn't half-myth at this point.

Yet there she was, voluptuous with dark red lipstick painting overly thick lips. She looked at him almost maternally, but with a smile that didn't touch her eyes. She looked to be in her late forties, but Cordray knew she was in her mid-sixties. Yet there were no wrinkles, no frown lines marring her porcelain skin, and her hair was pulled back into a tight bun that was tucked inside a smaller crown. Her angular cheekbones made her cheeks sink in, giving her whole face a narrow aesthetic. King Hubert had been captured in photographs with many a regal and imposing expression, but they all paled in comparison to his older sister's presence that exuded pure wickedness.

When he was brought in, she stood from what could only be described as a throne in the center of the long room that, even aboveground as they were, still felt cold, much like the concrete room below he'd been locked inside.

"Hello, Cordray. How lovely to finally meet you." Her voice was low and sultry when she spoke, and despite his fear, an errant thought passed through his mind that she would make a fantastic jazz singer.

Cordray did his best to stand straight as Dustin and Jared released him. He wondered where on earth he was, but didn't think information like that would be handed over to a flight risk. He didn't respond to her greeting, but stood tall, a slight sneer on his face.

Malaura waited for him to speak, but when he didn't, her smile melted. "I've heard great things about you. Adam Fontaine called a doctor to get his burn marks looked at after your attack, and I must say, I was impressed when I read the report. Such raw talent. There's a power and control to your electricity that most study years to achieve, but never do." She paused, sizing up his sneer with appreciation. "You're gifted, that's for certain. What a waste, that you didn't grow up with anyone to show you who you are." She shook her head. "What I could've done with power like yours. And to think, the Chancellor wants to shut you up and shove your abilities in a closet to rot."

When Cordray still didn't respond, Dustin pushed him forward. "The queen's talking to you."

Malaura came down from her elevated chair and slowly circled Cordray, as if daring him to flinch from the intense scrutiny. She was tall – taller than him, even, by a handful of inches. She had long, pointy fingernails that were painted to match her cherry lips. "But I would never shut you away, as if your power is something to be ashamed of. If you were mine, I would parade you around for everyone to see."

Cordray fought the urge to roll his eyes, and tucked his hands behind his back, standing at attention to avoid fidgeting. He wanted to get back to Rory. If she was in her coma, then only he could wake her. He could picture Leah's pinched expression, and the Chancellor's tearful eyes as they looked down at their daughter. He could see Benjamin beating himself up, though everyone would swear there was nothing he could've done. Cordray even felt a pang of sadness for Prince Henry's plight, knowing that for all of his jokes, he cared deeply for his few friends.

Perhaps it was because he'd dealt with Remus more often through their time studying, but he saw his tutor's face clearest of all – his head bent over Rory's hospital bed, and a vacant expression on his face. He'd sacrificed five years off the tail end of his life to give Rory this chance. There was a commitment there that transcended most familial ties, probably because they worked together, went to family functions together, and studied side-by-side almost every evening.

And of course, Cordray was stuck who knows where,

talking about politics he couldn't have cared less about. The only ability he cared about right then was the one that would enable him to wake Rory.

Malaura moved behind him and brushed her fingers along the small of his back, causing him to stiffen. "Do you know what my Pulse is?"

Cordray said nothing, deriving pleasure from her frustration at not being able to draw him out.

She leaned in over his shoulder from behind, as if revealing a secret, but everyone in the magical world knew her confession. Her lips tickled the shell of his ear, and he tried to suppress a shudder. "I can absorb others' Pulses and make them my own. It doesn't last forever, mind you, but it's enough to make me the key that can unlock many opportunities for the Lethals who have been so carelessly cast aside." She moved to his left and ran her hand over Cord's chest, practically purring as she touched him how she pleased without permission or apology. "You're on the pill, though, so I can't tap into you yet. Pity." Then her tone turned sharp in Jared's direction. "Take him back to the holding room until the pill wears off."

Cordray began to panic at being locked away, so he opened his mouth. "I don't belong here. No matter what you want, your politics have nothing to do with me."

Malaura stiffened and held her hand up in Jared's direction to stop him. "Nothing to do with you? Don't you understand what they want to do with all of us? The moment you ask them for the pill, they've registered you in their system. They want to strip us of our magic." Her nostrils flared as her temper climbed.

Instead of biting back or caving, Cordray kept his voice low. "You've got to know that attacking the Chancellor's daughter isn't the way to convince legislature that we're okay left unchecked. It's the stunt you and your people pulled that'll push everyone closer to the edge."

"If we don't fight back, they'll do as they please. Right now the pill is optional, but it's a swoop of a pen away from being mandatory if my insufferable brother wills it. Can you imagine? From the time children are old enough to demonstrate magic, they'd have it quickly stripped from them! They won't be given the chance to prove they can be trusted. The choice will be made for them." She moved to stand in front of him and motioned to his form. "Imagine if your father hadn't spun that story about your mommy dying because of faulty wiring in the house."

Cordray's spine stiffened, his heart clenching in his chest at the secret that plagued him. "You don't know what you're talking about."

Her fingernails traced up and down his arm, as if it thrilled her to be near someone so deadly. "Do you think you're the first child whose parents tried to hush away problems with lies? Had you been found out, it could've been jailtime for you for the rest of your days, not to mention a mandatory pill that's given to every Lethal in lockup. And yet, look at how well you turned out. You found a way to self-regulate with your gloves. You're why we need to be given the choice."

"And *you're* why we won't be given one," Cord argued. "It's your attacks that set us all back."

Malaura lowered her chin in a slow seethe. "You're a Lethal, Cordray. No matter who you're sleeping with, you're one of us, not them. The Chancellor isn't coming for you. In fact, he'll be glad to be rid of you. Having a Lethal so taken with his daughter?" She let out a slow chortle. "I would send you back just to watch him explain that humiliation to the people. The precious daughter who lived for so long on borrowed time, one touch away from being electrocuted for the remainder of her days."

"I would never hurt Rory. The Chancellor gave me that pill to help us both."

Her upper lip curled in distaste. "People say I'm evil because I welcome in the cast-outs, but it's my brother who's the tyrant, doling out that pill. He's forcing scared and confused victims of fate to lessen themselves so the world can feel bigger in his tiny mind."

Cordray had never met the king, but recognized a decent headline spin when he heard it. "So you poisoned the Chancellor's daughter, abducted me against my will, but yet you stand here, preaching all about the power of choice?" Cordray couldn't hold back his eyeroll any longer. "You're an idiot."

Fire flared in Malaura's eyes. She stomped over to Jared and palmed his face with an anger that made

Cordray wish he hadn't opted for the flippant insult. Jared's arms flailed out, but he didn't push her away. Instead, he moved with her as she stalked over to Cord, her free hand darting out so she could grab his arm.

Cordray made to shake her loose, but before he could, a current rushed through that stopped him in his tracks. He'd never experienced a heart attack before, but he imagined this might be what it felt like. Pain seized his chest in a way that scared him. He cried out in shock, wondering if this would be how he died. His left arm began to grow heavy as Malaura's look of determination mutated to a sneer. "Do you think you can speak to me however you wish? Do you understand who I am? *I* decide who lives and who dies. I don't wait for the law to be fair. I break what needs to be broken, and I won't have you insulting me while I fight for all of us!"

When she released him, Cordray fell to his knees, clutching his chest as he willed his heartrate to hold steady. He glanced up at Jared, who remained expressionless at being so thoroughly used.

Malaura reached down and cupped Cordray's chin. "Do you have anything to say to me?"

There were so many things Cordray wanted to say, but he knew none of them would be all that helpful. "You'll be Queen of the Dead if you solve your problems like that." Then he gathered enough gumption and spat in her face, making it clear that no matter what she wanted, he wouldn't comply.

A BEASTLY KISS

"It's the beeping," Leah commented. "It's making all of us crazy. Benjamin, when was the last time you ate anything?"

Benjamin tilted his head at Leah, mildly amused at her mothering. He'd lived with the family for twenty-five years, and she'd never stopped treating him like he was her son, even though they weren't too far off from each other in age. "The last time I ate was the last time you did." His hands were tented in front of his lips, his shoes up on the edge of the hospital bed, and his elbows resting on his thighs. "I didn't think she'd still be here four months after the attack."

"She's breathing on her own," Leah said for the sixth time that morning. "That's promising."

"Promising that Remus' counter-curse held up, sure,

but no one's been able to find Cordray yet. I feel like I should be out there with them, searching."

Leah shook her head. "It's best you're here. You're her guard, and you're the only person I trust to watch her for us."

Benjamin let out a disgruntled "pfft". "You shouldn't trust me. She got attacked on my watch. I shouldn't have taken her to Cord's cabin. We should've gone anywhere else. Stefan's idea of holing up in the palace would've been better."

"Then King Hubert would also have been in danger."

"We should've left a day earlier."

Leah placed her hand on Benjamin's. "Enough. We all knew this was coming. There's nothing you could've done." Leah stood over her daughter's bedside and fluffed the pillows, taking care not to ruffle the comatose girl's hair. "She looks like she's sleeping." Leah ran her fingers down Rory's cheek, tearing up yet again. "My beauty. I remember the day she was born like it was yesterday."

Benjamin put his feet on the ground and frowned at Leah. "Don't you start with that again. You're going to get all emotional, and I'm telling you, I can't take it today. I'm barely holding it together."

Leah paid him no mind, lost in her memories. "She was perfect. I know every mother says that, but it was true about Aurora. Not a thing I would've changed, not even the sleepless nights." Tears fell down her cheeks in a steady stream, as they did every day around this time. "I would give anything for her to keep me awake now! Did I tell her I loved her enough?"

Benjamin couldn't tame his smirk. "Only every day, several times a day. Rory knows, Leah. She's still in there, remember. The nurse said we should talk to her as if she's in the room, so she'll remember to come back to us if her body gives her that option."

"But she won't come back until Cordray wakes her, and we can't find him!"

Benjamin shushed her gently, and rose from his chair to take her hand. He stayed by Leah's side until she calmed down, assuring her as often as she could hear it that somehow Rory would be alright.

He didn't leave the hospital when Leah's guard came to pick her up and take her home. She had political duties to attend to, but Benjamin did not. So he remained by Rory's side, sleeping there every night, even when the nurses tried to kick him out. Leah's guard could Pulse Compliance into people, so he did what he needed to get Benjamin permission to stay by Rory's side.

When Benjamin was alone with her, he uncoiled a fistful of her hair from under her head and checked the door to make sure it was shut. He'd hated braiding her hair when she'd been a child, but she'd loved wearing her long black locks in two braids on either side of her head.

"There you go, talking me into things you know I don't want to do," he chided the sleeping woman, as if it had been her idea for him to twist her hair in the hospital room. "If anyone asks, I'm telling them the nurses braided your hair."

When he finished, he sat back and pulled his book off the nightstand, opening it to read aloud to her. "I know you don't like my Westerns, but it's my turn to pick. You made me sit through Goldilocks and the Three Bears so many times, I had the book memorized. This is a drop in the bucket, kiddo." He flipped to the page he'd left off at the night before. "I'm hoping that you'll hate it so much that you'll sit straight up and tell me off for making you sit through the longest story of your life."

He sniggered at what he inserted in his mind to be her internal groan, but stiffened when the door opened. "Adam? What are you doing here?"

Adam's beastly face made him less likely to travel in the daylight, but it had been four months since Rory had fallen asleep, and he hadn't been by. Oh, he'd sent flowers and food for the mourners, but he hadn't stopped over to see the only woman who'd remained in his life. He scowled at Benjamin. "I wasn't expecting you to be here. It's after visiting hours."

Benjamin stood, but didn't extend his hand, knowing Adam wouldn't take it. "That's the thing about being her guard. I get to bend all sorts of rules."

"Get out. I need a minute with her."

Benjamin tilted his head at Adam. "You want to try asking that again, Son? Convince me why I should leave her alone with you."

"I'm her friend, and I need a minute with her."

Benjamin looked at Adam appraisingly. "A friend, eh? I've seen her friends show up here. I've seen her family. I've seen every single one of her employees come to pay their respects. But I haven't seen you come by yet. I have no idea why you're here now."

Adam snarled and threw his arms out to the sides after he set his leather satchel on the floor. "You want to watch, so I can give you a show? Do you really think I'll allow that?"

"A show? What are you talking about?"

"The curse! She asked me to… And Henry said he already tried, but it didn't take. I know it has to be Cordray, and I know we're not in love, obviously. But she made me promise I'd try to wake her."

Benjamin folded his arms over his chest. "So four months later, you finally got around to it? You are without a doubt, the most selfish man I know."

"I told you to get out. I can't imagine you being so obtuse as to need to hear instructions twice."

It wasn't Adam's surly nature that gave Benjamin the urge to stretch his legs out in the hallway, but the fact that he was willing to try anything to rouse his charge at this point. "If you're Rory's true love, I'll pucker up and kiss you myself."

Adam snarled at Benjamin and shoved him out into the hallway, shutting himself in the room with the only woman who loved him enough to stick around.

He ran his hands through his hair four times, silently asking himself again what exactly he was doing here. He closed his eyes, and then opened them to glare at Rory, who still lay motionless in her bed. He'd paid someone to deliver flowers and secretly install a tiny security camera in the room so he could keep an eye on her remotely, but Benjamin had been right. Four months wasn't exactly punctual for a first in-person visit. He'd been hoping Cordray would show up, but as the weeks ticked by, he began to lose hope that the man who'd electrocuted him was still alive.

Though he'd watched Rory on the camera, she was thinner in person. She'd always been a waif, but four months of intravenous nourishment had left her a hop, skip and a jump away from positively boney. She'd always been a little pale, but there was no hint of color to her cheeks anymore.

"This is stupid," Adam lectured her with a scowl. "You know this won't work. But of course, here I am, suckered into following your orders, like I'm some servant you can ring up for whatever favor you like." He paced the room, nervous that he was in this position, and that no one had been able to wake her.

She'd been good to him, despite everything. Though she didn't understand all the fractures in his mind, she accepted him – broken though he was. She'd loved him back when he was whole, happy and foolhardy as well. He wanted to fight her on this, but it was the only thing she'd ever asked him for.

"Fine, I'll do it. But it won't work, so don't say I never said 'I told you so,' because I did."

Adam hadn't kissed anyone in nearly a decade, and worried he'd forgotten how. As he leaned over, he remained frozen, his mouth inches from hers. His eyes closed, and for a solid three seconds, he allowed himself to hope that his kiss could break Rory's curse. He touched his forehead to hers, wishing with everything in him that life could be simpler. He didn't want to hear the voices that haunted him in his castle. He wanted his normal face again, which he'd taken for granted back when he'd been a spoiled young man, manipulating those around him with a dashing smile as he saw fit.

If love was a thing he could feel, Adam felt it for Rory and Henry alone. No one else had stuck by him after the years of him pushing everyone away. Though truthfully, he hadn't had to push all that hard. Most of his friends had been superficial - a tragic flaw that was mostly of his own making. Henry and Rory had come to visit him when it became apparent he needed professional help. They hugged him when he yelled at them. A few times a year, they even made it a point to force him to leave the castle he'd sequestered himself inside.

They loved him, and however capable he was of harboring those same precious feelings, he did only for Rory and Henry. Though he could never see himself writhing in the sheets with the girl who'd tagged along with Henry and himself on many an adventure growing up, he hoped the steady rhythm of their solid friendship would be enough to set her free.

Adam had scar tissue over his top lip that made the skin puff out a little, and it was covered in facial hair that every year started to feel more and more like fur, giving him his ever-popular nickname of "Beast". His canine teeth were elongated to the point of him having to make a concerted effort not to cut her when the dreaded moment finally came. He hadn't kissed a single soul since he'd been deformed, and wasn't even sure he remembered the mechanics of a subject he'd once dominated.

But there she was – the only woman who believed in his redemption enough to love him. The better man she cherished was nowhere in sight, yet still she held firm to her hope. Dainty though her hands were, she'd always kept a tight grip on her belief that fate could be changed, and that he was somehow capable of goodness. The three of them had the kind of loyalty that was the stuff of life-long friendships, but true love seemed to be a different thing entirely.

Her lips were soft, thanks to the fluids they were pumping into her. He turned his head on an angle to compensate for his puffy upper lip, tucking his fangs beneath, but the kiss was still horribly awkward. Anger flared up in him that she'd forced him to know what it was like to kiss with the deformities that had taken over his face, but he tried to be brave as the last vestiges of hope began to fade. What little optimism had been planted in his heart started to shrivel and choke as he kissed her again, smacking his hand on her bedrail in frustration as he grew more desperate to make this work.

Adam lost count of how many times he kissed his best friend, losing hope as the minutes ticked by with no marked change in her besotted state. When he began to taste a stale rust, he realized with self-loathing that he'd accidentally sliced her lip with his problematic overlong canines.

When he finally pulled away, he was surprised to find condensation misting his eyes. Immediately, he was cross with her for forcing the emotion from him. But he was enraged with himself for hoping – a bad habit he'd cast aside long ago.

There was no point in being angry with her as he pulled a tissue from the box on her nightstand and dabbed at the dot of blood on her lip, but he unleashed a torrent of lectures anyway until he'd exhausted himself. Then, plopping down in Benjamin's chair, he snarled at the old paperback Western the guard had been reading his charge. "You don't want to lie here and listen to this insipid book. If you're going to insist on lounging around all day and night for months on end, your head will at least get filled with something useful." He glanced at the door to make sure it was shut, and then reached into his leather satchel that he'd left on the floor. "If you don't like

Alexandre Dumas, well, then you're stupid." He flipped to the page he'd left off at, about a third of the way in. "And I'm not recapping what you've missed. If you wanted to know, you should've read the book yourself. It's centuries old, Rory. Centuries. Don't tell me you haven't had the time." He grumbled a little while longer, as if she had sighed her exasperation over his choice in classic literature.

When Adam began to read, his shoulders relaxed and rolled back. The knot that felt constantly lodged in his sternum loosened, and he breathed easier. It was the rhythm of the old language that soothed all that ailed him. He ached inside – a deep, guttural pit of despair that he'd learned to live with over the years. Yet in the dusty pages, Alexandre Dumas soothed him.

As he read aloud to Rory, he hoped that same comfort would cover her, as well.

27

PUSHING THE LIMITS OF MAGIC

"Again!" Jared shouted, hoisting Cordray up from the floor for what felt like the hundredth time that morning.

"You don't understand how my Pulse works. I can't shoot out electrodes at a target. I have to touch someone with my bare hands for anything to happen."

Jared was immovable, his expression never veering from the soldier who always did as he was told. "If the queen thinks you're capable of breaking the laws of magic, then you'll do it."

Cordray scowled at Jared and shook his arm off once he was on his feet. "What about you? Can you throw your Pulse? No! This isn't even possible. She even said no one's ever done this before! What makes you idiots think I can do this?"

Jared never argued more than was necessary. He stood

back and pointed to the bullseye on the other end of the concrete room Cord had been locked in.

Cordray obeyed, but he had little frame of reference. He'd never heard of anyone casting their Pulse without the use of touch. He knew it couldn't be done, but somehow, he now had to figure out how to accomplish such an impossibility.

Cord stared at the bullseye across the cold concrete room and raised his palms, his nostrils flaring as he tried to do as he was instructed. Three whole minutes of him gritting his teeth as his face tightened produced nothing – the same result he'd had every day thus far. Malaura only came by once a month to the bunker, he was told, and she would be most displeased if, once again, there was no progress to report.

Jared never appeared hopeful or frustrated. He was stoic – stuck in the bunker, which didn't seem to affect him any more than being out in the field under the sun might. He punished Cordray for not performing the task, which was how he ended every night, and then left the prisoner to lick his wounds in the dark.

There was a hole in the floor that served as the toilet, and meals that came two times a day. Other than that, Jared and Dustin were the only interaction Cordray was granted on a daily basis. Dustin was at least amiable and relatively chatty. Jared was a brick wall with absolutely no personality.

Cordray lost count of the days he'd been locked up, but

didn't lose hope that he would find a way out and get back to Rory. He'd almost escaped four times already, but was caught and punished with tortures that only enforced in his mind that he would never join them. The more they beat, suffocated, waterboarded, and attacked his internal organs, the more concrete Cordray's will became. He spent his spare time doing pushups when he was left alone in the room, planning and preparing for when the next opportunity for escape arose.

He'd surpassed the pleading and panicking portion of his imprisonment, and skipped right to plotting, which turned out to be a far more soothing color on him. When he'd escaped the first time, they'd broken his leg. The second time had been his arm. He knew he'd been incarcerated for at least eight weeks, because the medic they had onsite commented that it had been as long when they removed the cast from his wrist. And that had been who knows how long ago. His leg was mostly fully functional at this point, which only worried him more over how much time had passed.

Cordray pushed at the ground, repeating his calisthenics for the fourth time that day. He wanted his repaired arm up to snuff, without any weak points on his body when his next window of escape came about. He'd already killed seven of their people, which, he reasoned, was their own fault for taking him off the pill and trapping him like a dog. He'd gone his whole life trying not to harm anyone, and only a few months spent with the Lethals had him murdering. He tried to talk himself through the guilt, but it stung him all the same.

Cordray was sweating as he switched from pushups to sit-ups. When he'd been a boy and just discovering his ability, he'd only been powerful enough to kill a few bugs and give people a painful shock. When his parents had suggested gloves, his inner turmoil relaxed. He could be normal again and not worry about hurting the people he loved. Now that he was separated from them, and he didn't have the buffer of the pill, he felt exposed and a little unhinged.

That night, however, Cordray went to sleep with contentment ironing out the worry wrinkles he'd worn for too many months. Jared had socked him in the stomach a few times, and he knew his lip was bleeding, but he smiled all the same.

In the darkness, Cordray stretched out his hand and practiced sending a spark of electricity from the center of his palm into the hole in the middle of the floor. The grueling training had worked, though his keepers didn't know it. He'd endured the beatings, the suffocations and the torture, knowing that he could make it all end if only he revealed the evolution in his ability. But his power would never belong to them. It was his, and he knew just how to use it.

When Malaura came for him again, he would be ready.

28

CORDRAY'S PLAN

The rumble of the trucks as they pulled up to the bunker was the only thing that marked thirty days passing. Malaura came once a month to check on his lack of progress and "motivate" him some more. He couldn't imagine what she did with the rest of her twenty-nine days in each month, but she'd been something of a ghost to the world, so whatever it was, at least she was keeping the hazards of it away from the public.

Cordray sat up as if his spine had been spring-loaded, ready and waiting for this very moment. He stretched out his fingers and renewed his promise to himself that he would return to his life – that he would return to Rory. He pictured her face, ready and waiting for him as she always was. He vowed to buy her blouses with a little color in them, now that he knew her reasons for wearing all black and gray had more to do with self-flagellation over not having magic than mere preference. He wanted to take her out somewhere nice and sweep her off her feet. She'd been treated to mansions, castles and a prince courting her, but Cordray was determined to top all of that by actually loving her how she needed to be cared for, celebrating the parts of her she tried to hide out of shame. Maybe he couldn't buy her a mansion, but he had enough to pay for materials to build an extension onto his cabin. He was already making blueprints in his mind to construct a bedroom for Benjamin, and an extra for... the future. If she wanted a life in the city, he would use that money for a down-payment on a home nearer her office.

Cordray had never entertained thoughts like that about anyone, and knew better than to let Rory slip through his fingers. He wouldn't let any obstacle stand in his way, even if those obstacles had fractured his bones and tried to break his spirit.

He laid back down when he heard Jared's boots tromping down the hallway with Dustin's lax gait sliding behind. Cordray let his jaw go slack and closed his eyes, trying to look as lifeless, limp and pathetic as possible. It wasn't too far a stretch. If he wasn't so focused on getting home to Rory, he might not have held onto sanity this long. But they didn't need to know how lucid and strong he still was. That part would be a surprise.

The keys jangled in the door, and the sliver of light opened into a whole slice that fell over his face and forced a whine of discomfort from him. Though he craved the newness of light by morning every day, it was still painful when he spent so many hours in the windowless pitch-black basement.

"On your feet," Jared ordered. When Cordray's movements were sluggish and unfocused, Jared and Dustin each took an armpit and hefted him up. Each morning, they fitted him with rubber cuffs that stopped all chance of an electric current moving through his fingertips, so they could move him as they wished.

Jared took a water bottle from the tray Cordray refused to touch (he'd fallen ill due to tainted food a few days ago, and couldn't risk any sickness today), and splashed a little cold water in the prisoner's face to revive him. "Time to show the queen what you can do."

Dustin held onto Cordray even after Jared released him. He slapped the prisoner on the shoulder, as if they were old friends. Though he'd been part of the incarceration, Cordray couldn't help but sympathize. When Cordray had felt the sting of ostracization, he'd found his home in the woods with nature. Dustin's big mistake was wandering into the wrong group and finding his home with Malaura.

"I can feel it. Today's the day, brother. You'll show the queen all you can do, and she'll forgive you everything. You'll be her new favorite, that's for sure." There wasn't a hint of jealousy in Dustin, only admiration. Cord wished they'd met under any other circumstances.

Though Cordray was ready to pounce, he let drool fall

from his slack lips, completing the picture of the pathetic prisoner who'd long since lost any semblance of usefulness. He let out a moan, and let his left leg drag slightly to exaggerate any hints of pain that might be passable from a mostly healed broken leg. He could run on it just fine, but they didn't need to know that.

Cordray kept his head lowered as he leaned heavily on Dustin, but he listened to every sound that echoed. He knew from his various failed escape attempts that there was no way out that he could find to the east or west ends of the building. There were at least ten men in the bunker when he'd tried to escape the last time. There were always a handful more that accompanied Malaura when she showed up to note the prisoner's lack of progress. Some were the more stoic ones like Jared, but others had a greedy gleam in their eyes, hungry to let loose on the new guy.

Cordray waited for the grandstanding, knowing how Malaura loved to tease her food before she devoured it. She moved from her throne and snapped her fingers at Jared, motioning for him to stand a few feet in front of the prisoner. "How very good to see you, Cordray. If there was one thing that would make my day, it would be that you've actually learned the one lesson we've set out for you. Your Pulse is more than the average person's, so I expect you to *be* more."

She wore a low-cut black dress that fell a foot past the floor, dragging when she walked. It was formfitting, and quite sheer in parts. It was designed to seduce men into giving up their will to her. Though she possessed much magic, the dress itself left no stone unturned.

Her painted, sharp nail scraped under Cordray's chin, lifting his head so she could take in his unfocused gaze. "Are you going to disappoint me today? I fear if you do, I may take it out on your trainers as well as you this time." She tsked him, as if she cared about the sodden state in which he'd come to her. "It seems as though they've been pushing you a little too hard. A boy's got to eat, right?" Her chuckle was low and throaty, and she leaned in to palm the firm planes of his chest, as she did at every encounter. Malaura relished being able to feel him up. She perused his hard body as she wished, caressing his dark caramel skin as if she had a right to do as she wished. Though he was always unresponsive to her, she delighted in his handsomeness all the same.

"Your majesty, we've reported that there's been no progress," Dustin began to fret. He pulled a dirty handkerchief from his back pocket and began to mop the beads of sweat from his brow.

Malaura paid Dustin no mind. "Take off his cuffs, Jared. I want to see what he can do."

Jared didn't hesitate, but caught Cord's eyes with a warning to behave and do his best. He stepped back with the rubber cuffs dangling in his fist, ready for his inevitable punishment for the failure.

Cordray had gone over this exact scenario thousands

of times in his head as he'd prepared for his final moments in the bunker. He needed to get back to Rory. Even if his kiss didn't wake her, he wanted to simply be near her. Her presence calmed the tornado of turmoil inside of him. He'd gone too many months without her gentleness that bred civility in complete and total monsters. He feared he would soon turn into the monster they were trying to make him, so he was desperate to return to her. He needed to find his heartbeat again. It felt out of sync, so far away from her smile.

Cordray lifted his hand and made a grimacing expression as if he was truly trying his best to accomplish the unattainable. His eyebrows pulled together as his upper lip curled in frustration. After a few noises of consternation, he lowered his hand and slumped his shoulders.

Malaura's heels clicked on the floor in an angry pattern he knew meant trouble. She was annoyed. She was frustrated.

It was exactly how he wanted her.

Malaura was most erratic in her fury, and went for the throat instead of the plan. She snatched at Jared and grabbed onto Cord's wrist. Cordray was prepared for his heart to seize in his chest, but this time, that didn't happen. It was Jared whose mouth popped open in a frozen "O" as Malaura stripped currents from Cord and Pulsed them into Jared to punish him for failing her too many times.

Cordray felt a small thrill of vindication when Jared

was rendered useless, struck with pain only he could inflict. He reveled in Jared's agony, permitting a dark smile to curve his features.

In that moment, Cordray knew that even if he escaped, they'd succeeded in changing part of him that was precious to the survival of a soul. He'd been so aware of the fight to keep his body alive; he forgot to make sure his soul came out the other end intact. There was nothing much for him if he came to Rory all twisted by Malaura. Though, at this point, he knew part of that was a done deal.

It was when Cordray started to smell something burning that he realized what Malaura had done. She'd used him to murder Jared (which, Cord had to admit, crossed his mind on many occasions). But being used solely as a weapon opened a door inside of him that he knew might never be shut again.

When Malaura released them both, Jared fell to the floor. A sad puff of smoke wafted from his lips, signifying that everything that had once been alive inside of him was now fried.

Malaura rolled her shoulders back and cracked her neck, smiling with satisfaction at the dastardly deed she'd orchestrated. "My, my. How deadly these Lethals are. If anyone comes looking for you, I think we'll keep Jared here as proof that you've gone off the rails. I've never seen anyone's Pulse as strong as yours. I killed him in almost no time at all, with barely any concentration! To have that coursing through my veins?" She smiled at him, eyes lidded as she shivered. "Oh, the fun we'll have together."

Her guards were all in various stages of shock. There's a certain amount of evil that's expected when one signs up to fight with the bad guy, but judging by the worried looks on their faces, Cordray surmised that Malaura had never turned on any of them in such an irreparable way before.

"Your majesty, is Jared... Did you kill him?" Dustin asked, horrified.

She glanced around the room with narrowed eyes, taking in their terror with a superior glint. "He failed me. Hopefully that will be a lesson for all of you. Fail me too many times, and risk my displeasure. Jared displeased me, so he's dismissed from my service."

Cordray listened to the conversations volley back and forth between her and her henchmen. He'd never seen them question her before, and it was just the confusion he needed to create enough chaos to stage his escape.

Malaura's fingers flexed when one of the men accused her of setting Jared up for failure. "No one can do what you wanted him to train the new guy to do – not even you! It's not possible! You killed Jared for nothing!"

When Malaura stalked over to the backtalker, Cordray didn't move more than a simple twisting of his wrist, so he could aim his palm at the man. The moment she touched her brazen henchman, Cord shot an electric current out that flashed a spark only as it zapped on the man's skin. He cried out, but the others didn't understand it as anything other than Malaura enacting her malicious desires onto her peons. To the others, it appeared as if she was shaking him, but only Cordray knew it was his current surging through the man. The electricity leapt into her body, freezing them together with enough electricity to keep her from alerting the others with an intelligible command.

Over and over, Cordray shot the man, amping up the current each time until Jared wasn't the only body smoking in the long, cold throne room. Though they'd all been hoping for it, no one other than Malaura actually expected Cordray would be able to cast his Pulse - murdering without a single touch.

There was a moment of hesitation when he realized two more people's deaths would now be on his head, but Cordray resolved himself to feel the remorse later, in the fresh air where even the darkest of sins had room to fly away.

29

THE EVOLUTION OF MAGIC

When Malaura fell, it was with a cry of elation that Cordray gave away his position of power. The henchmen were torn between tending to their queen, and charging the Lethal who'd taken down their fearsome leader.

Cordray didn't know what kind of man he would be after this, but he knew he wouldn't find out if he never made his way out of the bunker. His slack jaw snapped back into place, and his slumped posture became lithe and strong. His hands rose, and though he didn't want to fight them, he knew there was no other option. Even if they somehow agreed to let him go, the knowledge of what he could do would be out there, circulating for others to try. They wouldn't stop until he was studied and his abilities replicated, shoving Pulsing up to the next level of danger. It would be catastrophic if people had a wider tether to enact their wills upon others.

For the good of the world, no one could know what he was now capable of. He stood in front of the doorway, guessing that he could cut and run right now, and probably escape. But for how long? He knew that as much as he wanted to bolt, the madness needed to end today. Cordray shook his head, wishing there was a better solution, but understanding there wasn't one.

"Calm it down, Cordray. Put the cuffs on, and we'll go easy on you," one of the men said, picking up the rubber cuffs from the floor and tossing them to him.

The cuffs banged against Cord's chest, and then fell to the floor. "I think you'll all do what I say this time around. Dustin, put these cuffs on yourself. I'm walking out of here with only one prisoner today, and it's going to be you."

Dustin blinked at Cord, confused. "How long have you been able to throw your Pulse?"

"Put on the cuffs, or I'll electrocute you just as easily as I did your queen!"

Dustin jerked into action, obeying as the sweat dripped down his hairy temples. "What's the plan, Cord? You're going to fry them all?"

Cordray flexed his fingers and bent his knees, willing all of them to attack, so his conscience could justify the works of his hands.

When the first man took a hesitant step toward him, Cord didn't hold back. His abdomen tensed as he Pulsed out a current of electricity enough to light the entire bunker for a week. The man didn't cry out – his body was too locked down to manage the smallest of sounds.

The others shouted enough on his behalf. Though they'd seen Malaura go down in the same way, to watch one of their own breathe his last in the span of a few seconds shocked them all into action. Some of them charged him, while others backed away. It was a risk to touch Cord, but some of them were just kamikaze enough try it. Cordray felt his arm begin to burn when the man who could singe skin with a single touch grabbed him. But no sooner did the burning sensation make him cry out, did the current pass through and deliver a direct hit to the attacker's chest.

Over and over, Cord shot out currents, his aim growing more miserably off the mark as he was touched by Lethals who were desperate to take him down.

The biggest difference was that they had only their own lives to fight for. Cordray commissioned himself with the knowledge that Rory's life now depended on his survival, so he fought through the fire, through the broken wrist one of them delivered with a well-placed touch, through the pain, and finally, through the last man's end.

Cordray let out a noise of distress as the breath was knocked out of him when he was tackled from behind. He cried out when none other than Dustin bashed his forehead down on the concrete, dazing him, but not knocking him out.

When Cordray's warden knelt on his back as he tried to suck the air from his lungs, Cordray knew he had no other option. Though he didn't even know if it was possible to Pulse someone through one's back, and not through touch or throwing his Pulse, he spun fate's wheel and gave it a frantic try. The on-tap current Pulsed through his entire body, making him light up with electricity. He cried out as the current shot through his spine and up into Dustin. It was desperation that led to a second magical rule of nature being broken, but Cordray took no joy in the metamorphosis.

Dustin slumped to the floor after Cordray tipped the dead body off his back. He lay for a few minutes on the concrete, catching his breath and willing the world to stop spinning. Finally, he managed to get up onto his hand and knees, his chest heaving as he cradled his broken wrist to his chest. His skin had burn marks littering his forearms, but he didn't care. He could scarcely feel anything anymore. It was all clouded by the burning desire to get home to Rory.

So focused was he on getting to the home that always called to him, that he didn't do more than a quick surveillance of the room to check for partially moving bodies.

He didn't think to check for heartbeats – his own pounding too loud as he stumbled through the many hallways, and finally, out into the daylight.

30

UNHINGED ESCAPE

Driving toward the mansion was challenging with only one hand, but Cordray managed. When he hit the freeway, he found he wasn't even in his home state, but far from anything familiar. Unhinged as he was, he scraped at the skin on his neck to force himself to stay alert through the long drive in the stolen vehicle.

It had been so long since he'd seen the outdoors. It was all so bright, with clumps of snow marking the season, letting him know the world had indeed kept spinning without his participation.

He wanted to take a minute to appreciate his escape, but wasn't sure how big Malaura's infrastructure actually was. If more would be coming, he didn't want to be waiting around, unconscious and easy to pick off. He bit down on his finger to keep himself awake, but soon only the pain of moving his broken wrist was enough to keep him alert.

He wasn't sure where exactly he'd started out, but he hoped making a call to Rory's phone from the one he'd stolen off the body of a dead man would at least tell him where he was going. He knew he didn't want to be anywhere near the bunker when law enforcement showed up.

"Stay where you are!" Benjamin ordered him upon answering Rory's phone and hearing a few clipped sentences from the man they'd been searching for for months. "They need to take your statement and get you medical help. You sound deranged, Cord."

"I don't care about making a statement! Tell me where she is! The cops can follow me there." His voice slurred on a few of the words, due to his adrenaline plummeting, which combined poorly with his undernourishment and head injury.

"Pull over. You'll be no good to her if you drive off the road. You sound drunk."

"Not drunk. Where is she? Tell her I'm coming."

"Pull over, and I'll come and get you myself. You have to talk to the police. Everyone's been looking for you."

"You have?" Cord was stunned. He'd assumed they'd given up long ago.

"Of course," Benjamin's voice softened. "You belong with us."

Cordray shook his head when the road started to blur

in front of him. In the back of his mind he knew he should pull over, but he'd survived this far. He didn't want to get abducted again. "You can't leave her. I'll come to you."

"Stop your car and tell me where you're at. I'll send Remus to pick you up."

Cordray finally obeyed, but only because he had to. The world was starting to get blurry around the edges. "Hit my head," he murmured to Benjamin.

"Tell me where you are!" Benjamin roared, and in the background, Cordray could hear the purr of the town car's engine firing up.

A note of angst crept out of Cordray as the confession bubbled to the surface. "They're dead! I killed the Lethals. There wasn't any other way. Malaura, she's... Someone needs to come clean up all these bodies."

Benjamin swore. "How many of them had you captive?"

"A dozen? Maybe more? I got out, but I had to kill them to escape." The confession felt like breathing, but Cordray knew it would take more than that to cleanse his soul from the filth that felt caked into the crevices of his psyche.

Cordray glanced out the windshield and squinted up at the green sign overhead on the freeway. "Fairview in one mile. Exit 136. Black sedan. Dead bodies. Rory! Rory."

That was all he could get out before the edges of his periphery began to tunnel. He pulled off onto the side of the freeway seconds before the world he'd longed to see once more faded to black.

31

THE TEACHER AND THE STUDENT

ordray's dreams were blurry and strange. There were swirling colors and shapes that seemed to represent people, but didn't look a thing like them. He heard voices that echoed down from the heavens, but couldn't connect the voices to actual language until he strained to pay attention.

The tune of the voice was easy to pick out – Malaura had that way about her. When her words started to funnel down and put themselves in proper order, Cord stiffened. "Mine! He slaughtered too many people to walk free. You'll let me have him, or I'll come after you both!" She didn't sound her usual cruel and calculating; she sounded almost drunk, her speech slurring.

Cordray's heart seized in confusion. His lips parted to offer up a protest to the universe for messing with him so cruelly. *Malaura died. She was on the ground when last I left. The current I hit her with had to have been strong enough.*

"You're in no position to make bargains. Let him go, or you die. Are you limping? Is the great Malaura actually displaying weakness to us common folk?"

Cordray rallied at the sound of Benjamin's voice. Though he didn't particularly care for the fact that the stoic guard came with Rory as part of the package deal, in that moment, he knew he would gladly build the man a spare bedroom on his cabin if only Benjamin could get him out of this mess unscathed.

"Wake up, Cord!"

Cordray opened his eyes, but the world swam at a sickening pace. The colors and shapes began to blur into dripping lumps of clay that all seemed to want something from him. He felt his heels skip over rocks, and realized he was being dragged. Sharp nails dug into his armpits, piercing his skin and rousing him faster than the strongest coffee. The evening sky greeted him with a hearty cheer of "Get up and run!" so he tried his best to comply. His legs felt weighted and his arms clumsy, but he had one thing going for him that didn't require much effort on his part. Cord was heavy, and thick with muscle. It didn't take much for him to heft his body out of her grip, landing himself perched on three limbs on the side of the freeway.

Remus and Benjamin ran forward, the latter with his knife drawn and murder glowing in his eyes. Cord didn't understand how it was that she was upright, and well enough to drag him ten whole meters from the car he'd stolen fair and square. He'd electrocuted her with enough volts to make smoke billow from her parted crimson lips. There was no way he hadn't killed her.

Fear lit him up from the inside when the thought crossed his mind that perhaps he wasn't powerful enough to take down such a formidable foe. For all the interest Remus had shown in cultivating Cord's magic, praising him for its strength, Malaura had survived his best attempt.

Malaura was livid and growing desperate. "We have as much right to magic as you do! I won't stop until every Lethal knows the full extent of their power! My brother took my kingdom from me, but see? They flock to me, even when I have no crown!"

"Where are they now?" Remus countered, his chin raised in defiance.

Her drunkenness was painted with the brush of sweetness, as if she loved Remus without reservation, forgiving his betrayal. "Oh, my little lost boy. My favorite student. You ran away from me after everything I did to help you. Ran straight into your brother's clutches. How they must worship you after all I've taught you. It's not too late to come back. I forgive you, Remus."

Remus' chin lowered, and a cold snarl twisted his features. "You kept me in the dark. The light of day has no place for someone like you!"

Her syrupy disposition melted into a chilling sneer.

Malaura held out her palms to the men and began chanting something that made Cordray's blood run cold. He didn't know much about curses, but recognized a few of the Latin words easily enough. Everything in him screamed to stop her, to shove the words back in her mouth and stop her wicked influence once and for all. If nothing else, he needed to make sure she never cursed anyone again.

He had a hard time focusing his gaze, and worried about the damage a spark sent in the wrong direction could do. He grunted as he tried his best to rise to the occasion, but his strength was failing him, as it had so many times in the bunker.

Only this time, he wasn't alone.

Remus began chanting a different string of syllables with the same Latin, and as he stalked toward his prey, the snow began to melt. It was curse against curse, and the bursts of nature around them started to rebel. The ice-bedecked bushes that dotted the side of the freeway suddenly burst into flames, lighting Remus' path to her with a fury that seemed to emanate from his eyes. She'd messed with his family one too many times.

Today it would come to an end.

Cordray could see the determination. He could see the familial loyalty that was set in deep. He could see years of Remus torturing himself that he hadn't been able to completely undo Malaura's curse, but only offer a counter to it – putting Rory's life on hold instead of saving it completely. He'd sacrificed half a decade of his life expectancy for the chance that his niece might be saved. Malaura had cost him five years, and who knows how many sleepless nights. He was ready for her this time, unwilling to give her an inch of ground to stand yet another curse upon.

Benjamin wasn't willing to stand back and see how it all played out. He charged Malaura, a crazed fervor painting his eyes as he clutched his knife.

Despite her concentration on the spellwork, Malaura stomped her foot on the back of Cordray's head, and Cordray knew she wasn't just trying to keep him pinned down. She was readying to rake in his Lethal ability, to use it against Benjamin when they collided.

"No!" Cord howled, knowing that this last struggle would be the one that mattered most. With his last ounce of strength, he pushed up from the ground, faltering on his broken wrist as he did his best to part from her. It wasn't graceful, nor was it painless, but Cordray finally shirked away just in time for Benjamin to crash into her form.

It was a breath and a gasp when Benjamin sank the blade into Malaura's belly. She'd tormented his charge for too long, and no matter what, the battle would end this very night.

Relief flooded through Cordray when Remus fell to his knees as the last words of the curse he'd stored up for her died on his lips.

Cordray's world went from chaos and terror to suddenly still. The snow fell around him, tickling the tips of his ears as if to ask him what all the fuss was about.

Remus was thorough with his confirmation of Malaura's death, his hands pink from the icy freeze. "It's over," he breathed. "It's finally over."

Cordray's elbows shook as his body began to give up. He cried out for Remus, but that seemed to be all his body was capable of at the moment. He collapsed face-first into the snow, his last ounce of lucidity dedicated to hoping they would bring him home to Rory.

32

THE BROKEN MAN

An entire four hours passed after his last examination before Cordray was given the all-clear from the doctor to walk around. "Apparently, they take bumps on the head pretty seriously around here."

"Doctors are funny like that." Remus remained by his side through all the exams, making sure his student was given gloves until two pills could be procured to numb his magic. "You feeling alright?"

"I'm feeling like I need to get to Rory. Tell me where she is, Remus. I followed the doctor's orders, now tell me where she is."

Remus scoffed. "If you call trying to escape your hospital bed too many times to count 'following the doctor's orders,' then sure. You were the model patient. Or *im*patient, as it were."

"Hilarious. Don't you have a Foundation to run?"

"That's the thing about family emergencies. They sort of trump all the other things that once seemed so important. My team can handle things without me."

"Tell me where she is, Remus. We all know I'm the only one who can wake her." Cordray hung his head. "Seven months! I can't believe she's been in that bed for seven months."

"That's how long you were in captivity, Cordray. As much as I'm glad you want to get to her, the doctor showed me your scars. The Lethals really did a number on you."

Cordray frowned at his tutor. "I thought those files were confidential. What ever happened to the patient's privacy?"

"I told them I was your uncle." Remus met Cordray's gaze with a note of a promise blazing through. "When you were gone for so long, your friend wanted his condo back, so we moved all your things into my home. We have the same address now."

There were so many details Cordray hadn't thought of while he was locked away. "I didn't realize. Thank you."

"It was only a matter of time before you moved in. Benjamin doesn't do stress all that gracefully. Watching you and Rory is just easier if you're under the same roof. Rory stays at my house most weekends, so it just made sense."

Cordray frowned. "I don't need someone watching me. I'm a grown man."

Remus put his feet up on the mattress and leaned back

in the bedside chair. With his posture relaxed as it was, he looked far younger than his thirty-six years. "Ah, but that's where you don't get much choice in the matter. If you're with Rory, you're associated with the Chancellor, which means that if they want to get at him, they can use you to make him bend. A guard comes with the territory once you're in the family."

Cordray's mouth went dry at the very permanent role he'd somehow woken up in. "I can take care of myself."

"Benjamin will be thrilled to hear that, I'm sure. But it doesn't change the fact that you need a guard."

Cordray sat back down on the bed. Though he'd been anxious to get out of it to go see Rory, his body felt weighted all of a sudden. "There's no one left to come after us. I killed all the Lethals. Every last one of them."

Remus quirked his eyebrow. "If only that were true, and if only the Lethals were our only problems. You killed the Lethals who worked for Malaura who were there at that time. She's got sects of them all over the place. And there are ones who are just like you – Lethals all over who haven't sided with her. They might be totally fine out there on their own, or they might decide that they hate the Chancellor's encouragement for Lethals to take the pill, and come after him. It's an ongoing struggle, being in the family of a politician."

Cordray pursed his lips, and then jutted his chin out at Remus. "You aren't attacked."

Remus put his feet on the floor and leaned forward.

"Our community fears me. I'm the only one who was able to counter Malaura's curse. Even so, I've still been attacked eleven times over the years because of my brother's position. It is what it is. I believe in the chance my brother is trying to give people who've been marginalized by their Pulses. I know what I'm up against, and I watch out for Rory, who's always been in far more danger than me. Still, you should know what you're getting yourself into. They *will* come for you again." He tented his fingers in front of his chest. "And when they do, I'll be there."

Cordray's gloved fingers tightened on the edge of the bed. "Malaura's been confirmed dead?"

Remus nodded. "That's the thing about having people in high places on your side. My brother's quite thorough. Four coroners confirmed her death after I did."

Relief flooded through Cordray as he let out a breath that he hadn't realized he'd been holding in for who knows how long. "Thank you. I don't want Rory to have to worry about that witch for the rest of her life."

Remus tilted his head to the side. "You really love her, don't you. I mean, you just got out of a seven-month-long torture-fest, and all you've been able to talk about is getting back to her."

Cordray flexed his fingers inside of his gloves, looking down at the self-made prisons that brought him freedom and comfort. "Nothing else makes sense. I feel like I've changed so much that I barely recognize myself. I need her to recognize me, Remus. If she can still see me rattling around in here, then maybe parts of me still exist."

Remus bowed his head to respect the brokenness that a man goes through when he endures too much duress. When he lifted his head, Cordray didn't bother to hold back the hollowness In his eyes, and the bags beneath his lashes that made him look haunted and on edge. Remus leaned forward and handed Cordray a clean set of clothes he'd brought from home. "Get dressed, and I'll take you to her."

For the first time in over half a year, Cordray felt himself breathe. He was muscling through a broken rib, a fractured wrist, a headwound, dehydration, undernourishment, and too many old wounds to count, but now that he was allowed to see Rory, he convinced himself that he was a new man. Nothing would stop him from getting to Rory, to see if she could love the broken man he now was.

33

SLEEPING BEAUTY

*I*t wasn't just Remus, but also the nurses who insisted Cordray move about the hospital in a wheelchair. He hadn't gone through proper physical therapy from when his leg had been broken, so his gait wasn't all that steady. One spill, and his fractured wrist and busted rib would fall out of sync all over again. He was practically shaking with need to be near her, but Remus drove the wheelchair painfully slowly, as if to exacerbate Cord's last nerve.

"Maybe we should stop for coffee. You need anything from the vending machine?"

"I swear, if you stop, I'll get out of this stupid thing and bang on every door to find her myself."

Remus chuckled. "Well, we can't have that. You'll break that wrist all over again, and then where would we be?"

Remus strolled down a few more hallways, and then finally stopped in front of a door in a quieter wing of the hospital. Though it was brightly lit, it seemed to be a place not many people wandered. There weren't many emergencies in this wing, since most of the residents here were in comas. It was quiet, with a soft violin playing songs dripping with emotion overhead to soothe the two nurses at the station.

Remus smiled at them and popped Rory's door open, wheeling Cordray inside. The Chancellor and his wife stood, and Benjamin busied himself making space for the wheelchair. There were bursts of color from every kind of flower Cordray could think of. They littered the room with condolences and wishes for a speedy awakening. Still, with all the fragrant beauty, Cordray saw only Rory, wilted on her hospital bed, too many tubes keeping her body in stasis.

"Come on in, Son," Stefan said to Cord, waving him forward. "How are you feeling?"

Cordray gave a nod to the Chancellor, but his eyes were only on Rory. His life had been filled with such ache; she was the loveliest thing his eyes had viewed in over half a year. "I'm well enough to see her now."

Cordray couldn't tear his eyes from her. For so many months, he'd envisioned her face, replaying her laughter in his mind to give himself a distraction from his grim surroundings. Yet even in his most vivid imaginings, nothing compared to the real thing. She had no color in her face, nor life in her closed eyes, but her breathing held steady. She looked to be merely sleeping, and everything in him longed to wake her. He needed to confess his many sins to her. He needed to unload all the torment he'd gone through. He needed a safe place to rest his head, and in all of his years, he'd never met a safer place than Rory – despite the doom that often followed her around like a lost puppy.

Oh, how lost he felt. He needed her to find him in the darkness that seemed etched in too deep to ever go away.

His eyes misted over, and his voice came out a croak. "I tried everything I could to get back to her sooner."

Leah produced a near constant stream of tears since her daughter had fallen asleep, and that day proved no exception. She bent down and wrapped her arms around Cordray's neck, taking care with his broken body to be gentle. "We know, Son. We did everything we could to find you. You're here now, and that's what matters. You're safe, Cordray."

He bit down on his lower lip and willed himself not to break down at the maternal sweetness he'd been deprived of for far too long. He lifted his good arm and touched the side of Leah's face, keeping her cheek mashed to his for a few more precious seconds. "Say it again," he begged in a whisper.

Leah's tears touched on his skin. "You're safe, Son."

When he released her, she stood, and Stefan held onto Cordray's hand in solidarity. Cordray kept his eyes on Rory as he addressed the Chancellor. "Thanks for looking for me. There was a long time I wasn't sure anyone was coming."

Stefan cleared his throat. "We had teams of people who didn't stop looking until you called us. I'm ashamed to tell you that we were looking in the completely wrong direction. Malaura made sure she was seen far from where you were being kept. It led us on a rabbit trail that only kept you hidden longer. I'm so very sorry."

Cordray squeezed the Chancellor's hand. "It's over now." Then he cleared his throat. "Would you all mind if I had a minute with Rory? I know you want to be here the second she wakes up, but I need to talk to her first."

Though Stefan and Leah were hesitant, Benjamin and Remus shooed them out, leaving Cordray alone with their sleeping beauty. The room was painfully quiet, so Cord kept his voice low. "How'd it all get so messed up, Story?"

He slowly hefted his body out of the wheelchair and sat in the seat Leah usually preferred next to Rory's bed. He could see her better from this vantage point, and took a few moments to fill his vision with more and more of her.

"I know I'm supposed to kiss you and it'll end all of this, but there are some things you should know first." He reached over and twined his fingers through hers, bringing her dainty hand to his cheek. Her skin was soft, which was a welcome relief to the hardness he'd endured without her sweet presence. "A lot happened to me while we were apart. I'm not sure how much of this you've overheard, or even if you can hear me now, but before I try to wake you, I think you deserve to know who it is you're kissing."

Though it had been his idea to confess it all to her, now that he had the chance, the words felt stuck inside his throat. He swallowed a few times, and took a few deep breaths before the account of everything he'd been through in the past seven months bubbled out of him like bile and acid. He hadn't told the nurses more than they needed to know to do their jobs. He hadn't told Remus, Benjamin, Stefan and Leah much beyond what they needed to know to clear him of all murder charges under the label of self-defense. While he logically understood this pardon, something in him felt changed in an irreparable way. Good reason or not, now it would be known that he was a murderer – a mass murderer, no less.

He told Rory of each beating, finally allowing the tears to spill down his freshly-shaven cheeks. He relived it all for her, so she would know who it was that was holding her hand as if it was his only lifeline. When he confessed how he'd used his Pulse to murder his captors, the shame he'd kept tucked inside became suddenly airborne, floating around them for the flowers to turn up their petals at the stink of his actions.

"I killed Dustin," he confessed. "I didn't want to. I know he was a bad guy, but every now and then he cracked jokes and tried to make the whole thing not so terrible. I don't know why I can't shake it, but it's eating me up inside, Story. I didn't want to kill anyone with my Pulse. I tried so hard my whole life not to let that part of me hurt the world I was dumped into. But now it's out there. And the worst part is, I'm not sure I would've done it any differently if I was somehow given a do-over. I don't know what other option I had."

He hung his head, his chest moving in and out with a bit more grace, now that he'd unburdened himself. He moved her fingertips over his tears, pretending for a moment that she was comforting him of her own accord, and that she accepted this broken version of the man he now was.

"I'm sorry," he whispered. "I'm sorry for all I did, but most of all, I'm sorry I kept you waiting. I'm here now, though. I'm here, and I promise you, you'll never go to sleep without me again."

Then Cordray carefully lifted himself out of his chair and leaned over her, clutching her thinned hand between their chests. Their hearts were beating in the same rhythm, as it seemed they always had.

While others might doubt that a single kiss could wake the nearly dead, those people weren't witness to the love Cordray had for Rory, nor the storm of magic a humble kiss can unleash on the world. The only thing that could undo malice that was strong enough to bring forth a curse was the simplest and purest of all counter-curses – love.

As Cordray brushed his lips over hers, he knew before her eyes opened that Aurora's long sleep was finally over. He loved everything about his Story – the broken parts, the fragile parts, the strong parts and the gentle pieces that made him the perfect fit to wake his sleeping beauty.

34

VOWS

"You said I could wear a dress," Henry complained, turning sideways in the long mirror to admire himself in his tuxedo.

"I said you were my Maid of Honor. Where'd you make the leap that I told you to wear a dress?" Rory couldn't sit down. Her dress was too tight around the waist to allow for luxuries like sitting or bending.

"Adam should be here," Henry groused quietly. It was the third time that morning he'd said as much, but every time he glanced at the door and didn't see his best friend charging through it, he frowned.

"Adam is where he wants to be, which is moping inside his castle."

"He's being a baby about the whole thing. So you two had a fight. I feel like six months is enough time to get over it already."

Rory balked at him, her pink lips matching the roses in her bouquet perfectly. "He waited four months to try and wake me. That's not friendship. Adam's selfish, and I'm done trying to save him from himself. He's sulking, because he knows he was a shoddy friend, and I finally called him on it." She shook her head, and straightened out the heavy silk that belled out at her hips and brushed the floor with elegance. "I'm done babying him."

Henry shrugged. "But Adam's a baby. It's just who he is. I'm the charmer, you're the beauty, and he's the beast. It's how we work."

"Well, maybe that doesn't work for me anymore. I was in a coma for months before he even came to visit." Rory felt around with her toe for the tall satin heels that would make it so Cordray didn't have to bend too low for their first kiss as husband and wife. The shoes were hiding under her massive dress, and she huffed in frustration trying to locate them.

"Here, let me help." Henry knelt down on one knee, fishing under her gown for the errant shoes. Once he found them, he gingerly slid them on her feet, grinning up at her with a devilish gleam as he pressed a kiss to her knee just to see her blush.

Rory ran her fingers through his blond hair, softening at his sweetness that was always and ever purely him. "You came to see me the first day. Benjamin told me you kissed me every single day that first week, trying to wake me. That's friendship. You didn't leave me in limbo for four months before you decided to grace me with your presence."

Henry rose and wrapped his arms around her as best he could without crumpling her veil or wrinkling her dress. "That's just me trying to sneak one in on you, like I'm always doing. Adam is who he is. He was never going to be the one to wake you. You had to know that."

"I do, but even so, he visited me once in seven months. I've stopped by to check in on him at least once a month for the past decade!" She shook her head. "Well, no more. He can live and die in that filthy castle, for all I care."

Henry shot her a look of pure disappointment. "You don't mean that."

"Oh, I do. Adam didn't care if I died, Henry. That's not a friendship worth fighting for."

"You know that's not true. Things are harder for Adam than they are for the rest of us. You know he's not well."

Her pinched voice rose to a shout. "No, *I* wasn't well! I was in a coma, and I actually needed him to be strong for me for once, instead of me always picking him up off the floor."

Henry gaped at her, and then recovered. "You're so sexy when you yell at me. Tell me this white dress comes off easily."

Rory gave in to a smirk and lightly shoved him away, righting her veil in the mirror. "Cord gets to take this dress off me tonight, thank you very much."

Henry plucked his phone from his pocket and pulled

her close, snapping a shot of the two of them. They smiled wistfully at the photo, seeing the life that could've been, if only fate hadn't had a say.

"We look like we're the ones to be married," he commented quietly, his voice wistful.

Rory laced her fingers through his. "We do. I'm glad I get to keep you forever. The future king and the future Chancellor of Avondale."

Henry tucked his phone back into his pocket. "There's no one I'd rather spend the rest of my life beside. Will you be my Chancellor? Will you promise to keep me on task, and pick me up when I flounder?" His request had the note of a plea to it. He shifted to face her, holding their hands between them as if they were at the altar saying their vows.

"I do," she pledged. "Henry, will you be my fearsome and gentle king? Will you promise to listen to me and love me as you do Avondale, never turning your back on us?"

"I do."

The two shared a chaste kiss in the quiet of the bride room, sealing their vows that they would put Avondale first, and hold their friendship tight in their hearts.

Henry moved her palm to his cheek to warm her fingers, the two sharing a smile that bloomed from the preciousness of the moment that was purely theirs. "I think it's time, Rory." A gleam of mischief lit his eyes as his eyebrows danced to tease her. "I've got something brilliant planned for the ceremony."

Rory's face turned stony. "If you're thinking of fake proposing to me in the middle of my own wedding, I'll tear Cord's gloves off him myself and tell him to electrocute your testicles. I mean it, Henry. Behave yourself."

Henry sniggered at her wrath, as if he found her endearing instead of menacing. "I wasn't going to propose during your wedding. What kind of a selfish cad do you think I am? No, no, silly girl. I was going to follow you tonight and crash your honeymoon, so I could propose to you then. It's more intimate on a honeymoon, don't you think?"

Rory chuckled at her best friend's antics. "You actually would have a good chance at getting your balls electrocuted if you did that."

Henry rolled his eyes and batted his hand at her. "Cord's on the pill. He doesn't even need to wear those gloves anymore. He only wears them to punish himself, which I assure you, no one else is doing."

She ran her tongue along her teeth, unhappy that she hadn't confessed to Henry that Cordray actually needed two pills to mute his magic. Remus instructed them to keep that information private, but keeping secrets from Henry felt unnatural to her.

Rory straightened and cleared her throat. "Yes, well, that's Cord's choice, and I won't rob him of it. The gloves make him feel safer, so don't tease him about them."

"Roger that." When the doors opened, letting Stefan,

Remus and Benjamin in, Henry postured. "I think it's time, Glory."

When Rory raised her eyebrow at the new nickname, he explained, "Rory's too plain for a day like today, looking how you do. Today, you'll be Glory, and we'll all get to revel in your loveliness."

Remus gave his niece a slow, sweeping bow, paying respect to the long road it had taken her to get to this moment, and the sacrifice he had paid to make it all possible.

Rory reached out and placed her hand on Remus', her eyes burning with unshed tears that were threatening to fall. "All of this is because of you. I love you with all my heart, Uncle Remus."

He covered her hand with his. "Then repay me by living a full life. Every time you succeed, I feel the glow of it." He released her with a look of a brother letting his younger sister go off into the unknown. "Avondale and I live to watch you glow."

At his commission, Rory's shoulders rolled back, her chin lifting to make her posture regal and ready for the cameras.

Stefan extended his arm to his daughter, unwilling to fight back the tears that couldn't be helped. "If you're ready, I know a young man at the altar who's anxiously waiting for you."

Rory took her father's arm, but paused to wipe away the condensation from his eyes. He laughed at himself and shook his head. "If I'd known how wonderful you'd turn out, perhaps I wouldn't have worried so much."

"Maybe it's because of the worrying I turned out at all," Rory amended. "I'll be okay, Dad."

Stefan braved a smile and nodded. "Of course you will. Our nightmares are behind us." Stefan and Remus brought her veil down over her face, completing the perfect picture of the royal bride on her wedding day. With pink roses and the white lilies of Avondale clutched in her trembling grip, she followed Henry out the door, and into the narthex of the most ornate chapel in the land. It was where all the royals and important people of Avondale were wed – where Rory's parents said their vows.

After she was awoken, the story of how Cordray's love broke through Malaura's curse flooded the land. Every child wanted a repeat of the bedtime story, about how the mighty Cordray fought his way through a band of Lethals, breaking bones and fighting Malaura to the death so he could get back to his one true love. The single kiss that brought the Chancellor's daughter to life and set her dormant magic free was a grand feat that no amount of prose could capture, though not for lack of trying. Poets and bards from all over tried their hand at coining songs to be sung on Cordray and Aurora's wedding day. The entire kingdom wanted to be part of the miracle in which evil was defeated by love.

The harps played the traditional dirge as Henry walked out ahead of them, his sword in its sheath on his hip to complete the picture of the prince of the land. Every eligible woman in Avondale drooled for Henry – so much the more when he was in a tuxedo, doting on his best friend and playing the role of her Maid of Honor. Now that he was officially and publicly never to marry Aurora, his star status reached the stratosphere, attracting even the most reserved woman and drawing her eye with a charming smirk.

Remus walked out next – the mysterious man behind the Chancellor's rule who'd sacrificed a portion of his own life to see his family succeed. The people loved Henry, but they revered Remus, a few inclining their heads to him as he walked down the aisle.

King Hubert himself performed all the weddings of the higher-ups, and though he'd once expected to marry his son and Aurora when they'd been children together, the king smiled at Cordray, who stood to his left, knowing that Henry had never been taken with anyone the way Cordray was enraptured by Rory. He wanted that for his son, but knew it would take more than a betrothal to get the charming prince to settle down.

Before Rory could come around the corner to face the kingdom in the massive church, her father's footsteps froze. "Daddy?" she inquired, looking up at his worry when he didn't move forward.

"I... I... Forgive me, sweetheart. I knew this day would come, but now that it's here, I don't want to give you up! Tell me Cordray is a good man. Remind me of all the reasons why a father should be expected to let go of his daughter's hand."

Rory softened, smiling at his consternation. "Cord is a wonderful man. He's smart and caring, and after all he's been through, he still has a firm hold on his conscience. He's good to me, Daddy."

Stefan gulped a portion of his fear down. "I watched every step you took from the time you were a baby. Now that you'll be stepping out on your own without me? I can't bear it!" Stefan held onto his daughter's hand. "I need your Pulse, Aurora. Please."

"Uncle Remus told me I shouldn't use it unless there was an emergency."

Stefan's eyes widened. "The emergency is that I'm about to drag you out this door and drive away from this chapel until my heart calms down!"

Rory chuckled at her father's angst. "I love you, too." Her fingers brushed over his arm, and a wave of Peace flood through Stefan's skin. Though she'd been practicing with Remus and Cordray every day for months, the gift was still new to her, and apparently, it was one of the rarer ones that could turn lethal if left unchecked. Her first few times, she'd Pulsed so much Peace into Remus, that he'd lost consciousness for four hours. Since then, she'd learned to rein in the gift she'd waited her whole life to unwrap.

Stefan breathed more easily now, his shoulders lifting up and down with far less tension. "Ah, that's much better.

Thank you. You're getting quite adept at wielding your gift, you know."

"You can thank your brother for that. He's an excellent tutor."

"I've always said as much." He held his daughter's arm that wound under his elbow. "Shall we?"

The aisle was long, but the road to find true love had been infinitely longer for the two. Rory was poised and ready to say her vows when she held her husband's hands at the altar, but before any of that could be orchestrated, Cordray lifted her veil and pressed his lips to hers, skipping to the good part he simply couldn't wait for a moment longer. He cupped her startled face, his lips moving slowly with hers as the audience and many photographers chortled and swooned at the impetuousness of young love.

When the public had learned of their relationship, it took exactly one photograph for the world to fall in love with Cordray – for it was clear in the way he gazed at the Chancellor's daughter that he would never stop trying to win the heart she'd already handed him. His love for her fueled the public's adoration of the royal couple.

When Cordray finally sated his need to sweep her off her feet, he leaned in and whispered, "You will always be my favorite Story."

Rory's eyes were lidded as she slowly flitted back down to earth. "Tell me you'll always kiss me exactly like that."

"My kisses will always bring you back to life," he promised, pressing another to her cheek.

Years from then, Rory would remember scarcely little of the banners, flowers and ribbons that decked the chapel, proclaiming the joyous occasion. The shimmering spots of that day paled in comparison to the brightness in Cordray's eyes, which seemed to shine only for her. Though they'd been through much, their love was too great to ever be stamped out by the evil of the world.

Their first kiss as man and wife brought about a sense of romance and celebration to the entire kingdom. For if a former Deadpulse and a Lethal could find each other after everything life had stacked against them, then perhaps there was hope for them all.

The End.

Love the book?
Leave a review.

35

BEAUTY'S CURSED BEAST

*E*njoy a free preview of Adam's story in *Beauty's Cursed Beast* – a *Beauty and the Beast* Fairytale Retelling

"YOU SHOULDN'T HAVE A PULSE!" AUDRA EXCLAIMED AS SHE set the tea tray down on the stand. There were so many people milling about; she wanted to guard the delicate china cups, lest yet another of them chip. They were down to two-hundred-forty-four, which was barely enough for the crowd Adam had packed into the castle. Though, to be fair, they preferred shot glasses to tea cups.

Adam laughed at his housekeeper, his eyes dancing with mirth. "You're only saying that because you got stuck with putting people at ease as your Pulse. Mine's actually useful."

Audra leaned over and flicked his nose, just as she'd done when he was a little boy stuck in fits of petulance. "Yes. If only *you* were useful, as well." She was only half-joking, but she squinted her eyes at him all the same. "If you hadn't been gifted with the ability to persuade people as your Pulse, you wouldn't have a dime to your name."

"Oh, Audra. Persuasion is such an ugly summary of what I do. I merely strip away a layer of inhibition so they can see themselves and their options clearly. People love to be coaxed into doing things they'd otherwise be too scared to enjoy. Look at her up there. Isn't she a beauty?" He motioned to the mid-twenties woman who was dancing on the stage, stripping off one piece of clothing slowly for the viewers. "Now, if I used my Pulse on you, there's no way you'd end up on the stage doing a striptease for my friends, because you know who you are and what you want, which isn't that."

Audra shuddered. "Oh, my boy. These people aren't your friends."

Adam took a canape from her tray. "This girl wanted, in some buried part of her, to be up there doing exactly that. I just gave her a nudge."

"I believe that's the same logic used by drug-dealing scum."

"Oh, you." Adam batted his hand at the maid who could easily pass for his mother, and had served that function on many occasions when his own mother was away on her many social engagements. Now that his parents were deceased, Audra was one of the few chances he had at a conscience.

Just then, two guests came up to Audra to kiss her goodbye. Rory and Henry had been regular fixtures in the castle since they'd been children, but ever since Adam had taken the reins of the family fortune, they'd started leaving his parties earlier and earlier. "Goodnight, Audra," Henry said, kissing her wrinkled cheek that still possessed a bit of plump to it.

Adam frowned at his two best friends. "You're leaving already? Come on. It's my birthday! You can stay in your bedroom here."

Rory sank into Adam, her head resting on his chest. She looked dainty and frail in his thick arms, but he was always gentle with her. She was only fourteen, and by far the youngest in the castle. "I thought about that, but there are people up there making babies in my sheets. I think I'll just go home with Henry."

"You could always join them, you know." When his joke didn't garner a giggle from his best friends, but only stiff looks of disapproval, Adam released her with a frown of displeasure. "You never stay for the whole party anymore."

Rory glanced up at the stage, frowning at the impromptu strip show. "Can you blame me? This isn't exactly a proud moment for women."

Henry's arm coiled around her, as if to shield his friend from the debauchery. Though Henry was eighteen, he was much too old for parties like that, and took it upon himself to stay by Rory's side the entire night.

Adam frowned at Henry. "And you? What's your excuse for passing up on good whisky on my twentieth birthday?"

Henry shrugged, his blond hair still perfectly intact after the evening of dancing and mingling. "You know I can't be seen at events that devolve into this. My father wouldn't approve."

Adam scoffed with too much attitude to be overlooked. He'd started to do that more and more after the death of his parents. "Tell King Hubert that his son needs the royal scepter removed from his ass."

Henry tilted his head to the side, as if to silently ask if that's what Adam truly wanted to say. He paused, and Adam's bravado shrank marginally. Henry sighed heavily, and then brought Adam in for a hug. "I love you, even when you're an arrogant prick who forgets everything about the people he loves."

When the men released each other, Henry donned a wide grin for Audra. He always treated her as if the maternal affection she beamed was meant only for him. She pinched his cheeks to fill in the holes growing up without a mother had left on the boy. "Do stop by the kitchen on your way out. I made those cookies you like. Chef Bouche put them on top of the microwave."

Though Henry commanded many a room with his tall, built and handsome stature, he turned into a boy for her, bouncing on his toes with excitement at the doting. "Really? Did you put the peanut butter chips inside?"

Audra scoffed. "I'd like to know who you think you're talking to. I would never cheat my boy out of anything." She pulled him in for a hug and kissed his cheek. Instead of releasing him, she stole a moment to whisper in his ear, "Don't give up on Adam. He needs you."

Henry softened, savoring the hug that turned him from man into mischievous boy. "Never." Then he turned to Adam with a forced smile. "Happy birthday. I must say, that's the most unique wall-hanging I've ever seen." Henry's eyes darted to the large printout hanging directly across from the front door, so it was the first thing one saw when they entered.

The banished and feared former queen of Avondale, Malaura, had taken to sending Adam letters in secret, hoping to entice him to join her league of outcasts. The offers turned to love letters, one of which Adam had blown up and hung in the foyer for all to see. It was a shock for each guest when they entered, giving them guilty giggles at the scandal that Avondale's Most Eligible Bachelor was handsome enough to turn even the wicked ex-queen into a blushing schoolgirl.

Adam's grin widened as he glanced up at the poster with bravado. "Why, thank you. You should've seen the one I wrote her in return. Some of my raciest poetry to date."

Henry rubbed the nape of his neck. "Are you sure it's

wise to string along someone as powerful and vindictive as my Aunt Malaura?"

Adam rolled his eyes and pulled Rory into his arms, kissing her atop her straight, raven hair. Rory said nothing of the blatant poke at Malaura, and snuggled into Adam's side, closing her eyes as if she sorely missed her friend, even though she was currently holding onto him. "Happy birthday, Adam."

Audra's nose crinkled in distaste when the only two guests she enjoyed exited the party. "Your mother would be ashamed of you, Adam. Your father had that stage built for your violin performances, and this is what you use it for now?"

Adam's smile froze on his face at mention of his deceased parents, but it didn't fade. His expression twisted with a haughtiness he wore when challenged with integrity. "The violin doesn't amuse me. But this?" He leaned against the gold wallpaper that gilded the ballroom in a veneer of wealth and beauty. "*This* amuses me. Besides, I'm not strong enough to force anyone to do anything. All I did was strip her of her fear." He waggled his eyebrows at Audra. "She did the rest of the stripping all on her own."

Audra bit back her scoff of disgust, and set to pouring tea for the guests who wouldn't have noticed if she'd opted for the good tea. She'd selected the sub-par garbage from a bag instead, and no one said a thing. Most of them were drunk, as they were at all of Adam's monthly soirees. "Enjoy the cesspool you've created for yourself."

"I always do." Adam took the teacup and sipped the hot beverage with a sneer of distaste that she'd used the cheap stuff. "This is rubbish, and you know it." Still, he downed the cup, much to Audra's amusement.

"I'm glad you hated it. I laced your cup with a laxative."

Adam's thick chestnut eyebrows rose in alarm. He was highly desired due partially to his stunning chiseled looks, and partially because he'd inherited the largest fortune in history, along with taking over his father's profitable mortgage company. Though, he could've won the title on looks alone.

He eyed his tea cup skeptically. "You did what?"

"I'm tired of cleaning up bras from your floor. At least this way, there'll be no women coming after you for child support if you get careless. You'll spend your night in the bathroom, not the bedroom."

Adam glowered at her and placed his teacup on the tray. "You don't have to worry about things like that."

Audra patted his cheek, softening at his smile. "I always worry about you, you stupid, stupid boy."

Adam grudgingly kissed her cheek, and left her to join the others, who were hollering at the woman on the stage. She was down to her underwear and bra, which usually meant that it was nearing on midnight.

Audra yawned, but kept on her job, cleaning up the empty bottles and plates as she went. She caught Lucien's eye across the way, and the two exchanged a sad smile. Lucien's Pulse was that he could increase your happiness with a simple touch. He could have been put to great use in a nursing home or a preschool, but he was posted in the castle, shaking the hands of everyone as they walked inside. No matter what misgivings they'd had on their way in, the partiers left their caution at the door, smiling at the Pulse of happiness they were given upon entry.

Lucien sauntered over to her with a slight wickedness to his smirk that gave Audra a hint of a giggle. Though he was twenty years her junior, he always made it a point to dote on her. Even without Pulsing happiness into her, Lucien had a way about him that made everyone glad. His hips moved in a tango as he caught her up in a dance that made her feel young and enchanting, rather than the constant mother who, it seemed, would never be finished raising the man-child they'd all been entrusted to watch over.

"You look like you could use a little dance," Lucien pressed his torso to hers to coax a tango out of her. He was exactly her height of five-foot-ten, but had a longer nose than her modest one, and the ability to make a joke out of anything.

Audra kept up easily with the steps he slowed for her. "Oh, Lucien. I only dance for you."

Lucien had the kind of deportment that made everyone want to be his friend. While Adam had been blessed with stunning handsomeness (a gift from his far humbler father), Lucien had a smile that touched his eyes, and transcended mere superficial pleasantries. He looked into Audra's gaze and saw the sadness in the makeshift matriarch. "You're disappointed in our young man?"

"I don't want to be. I just can't shake how hurt his parents would be if they saw all this waste. Adam didn't used to be like this. He's barely turned twenty, and he's been given the wealth of a small country, and too much freedom without the life experience he needs to be able to handle it all."

"He's not going to run the company into the ground. He's like his father – brilliant eye for business. He just needs to get his head about him." Lucien looked as if he was about to say more, but the doorbell rang, which was his cue. He stopped the tango with an apologetic tilt to his head, resuming the duty that was truly beneath his talents.

"Mind your post," Bosworth chided Lucien, coming down from the stairs in his military jacket, which had fit him far better a decade ago. That was before Adam's father had offered him a salary he couldn't refuse. Bosworth checked his pocket watch and frowned. "The storm is getting more troublesome out there, and the guests are tracking mud into the foyer. See that Vivienne mops it up." Bosworth's pooched belly was sucked in, but it hardly made a difference to the strained buttons on the brown and red jacket. As head of the household staff, he made it his job to see to everyone else performing to Adam's satisfaction, no matter how depraved the parties became.

Lucien wasn't put off by Bosworth's haughty scolding, but blew the man a kiss, as he often did to throw Bosworth off his game. "Whatever you say, you old tease."

When Lucien opened the door, it wasn't one of the many twenty-and-thirty-somethings all dolled up for a night of debauchery at Adam's infamous parties. His eyebrows rose at the wrinkled old woman with a long nose and gnarled fingers. She wore a black cloak with the hood pulled over her head, shrouding her eyes in shadow. "The rain's really coming down out there. My car got stuck in the mud half a mile away, and you're the first house I've seen. Can I trouble you to make a phone call?"

"Of course, young lady. Come on in." Lucien doted on older women by referring to them as "young" ladies, which always garnered him a smile. He reveled not in using his Pulse, but in drawing out happiness in others without the use of magic. "Oh, it's really coming down out there. Here, let's get you into a chair and put a hot cup of tea in your hands."

The woman smiled at him, and took his arm as she trembled from the chill.

Adam stumbled out with two women, both drunk and cackling at something "hilarious" Adam had said. When the man of the house saw the old woman, he stopped short. "Go on up without me, girls. I've a matter to see to." He narrowed his eyes at Lucien, who pretended not to see the disapproval. "What is this?"

Lucien straightened, his deportment fitting in nicely

with the polish of the marble floors and the dust-free golden sconces that bespoke of good breeding. "This is a woman, and her car broke down. She's coming in to warm up while I ring for someone to assist."

"We have a dress code," Adam reminded his attendant, his chest puffing out to show off the expensive three-piece suit he wore. Though Adam was tall, muscular and built for chopping down trees, he'd been bred for real estate and taking over small companies. The tailor-made jacket was unbuttoned, but the blue vest beneath still made him look dapper and powerful. "She can wait in the stables. I don't need the guests seeing a sopping old crone standing in my foyer."

Lucien balked at his boss, whom he'd taught to ride horses and instructed on many a dance lesson. Now that Adam was an adult, Lucien wasn't "Uncle Lou", but rather the servant who was expected to obey at the cost of kindness. "Adam, surely you don't mean that. She's not bothering anyone."

Adam didn't act as if he cared when his guests disapproved, but his frown was more prominent when Rory, Henry, Audra, and now Lucien tried to control his behavior. "This is my home, and you're my servant, are you not?"

Lucien's jaw stiffened in time with his posture. "I don't think you understand the difference between a servant and a slave."

"I don't think you understand the difference between a paycheck and unemployment." Adam clicked his fingers at the old woman, not bothering with manners. "Out you go."

Lucien reeled backwards, breathless, as the old woman threw off her cloak, straightening her posture to reveal her true self. In seconds, her wrinkles smoothed, the signature royal blonde hue chased away the gray in her hair, she grew several inches in height, and her face shifted from an old hag to a beautiful woman in her fifties with an imperious look about her.

Adam gasped, and started in on a string of apologies when he recognized the woman as none other than the elusive ousted queen who'd cursed Rory as a baby. "Malaura?" Adam glanced behind him guiltily as his crass treatment of her private love letters to him framed his frozen form like a spotlight of doom.

Dread washed over Adam's features and he fell to his knees, knowing it wouldn't bode well for him to run at this point. She hadn't been seen in years, but whenever there were reported sightings, someone had walked away with a curse, if they'd managed to walk away at all.

"Run, Adam!" Lucien shouted, and then turned and darted into the ballroom to end the party and shoo everyone out through the back exit.

Adam was trembling under her intense scrutiny, humbling his posture so that he looked nothing like the haughty heir to the Fontaine fortune.

The sorceress looked down her suddenly slender nose and shook her head. "I've heard rumors of your pride, but never would've guessed the son of Moira and Peter Fontaine would've grown into such an arrogant prat. How I adored you from afar, but up close?" She glanced up at the private love letter she'd sent him, and a flicker of true hurt dashed across her pinched features. "Up close, you're quite disappointing. Beautiful, but utterly vapid."

"Malaura, I can explain."

She began to circle him, her black dress dragging out behind her. "Moira and Peter wouldn't have wanted this lifestyle for their boy. Your parents never sponsored my more interesting projects back when I sat on the throne, but I respected their firm command of their capitalistic empire nonetheless. They were good people who raised you far better than this." She tutted him, and then reached down to tap a pointy red fingernail under his chin to lift his head. "You're even more stunning than in your pictures." She bent over and caught his earlobe between her teeth and tugged, laughing at his shudder. "I prefer my toys to be pretty, and you're by far the most beautiful man I've ever seen. How I would love to take you home with me. Oh, the things I could teach a virile student like your-self." Her tongue darted out to wet her crimson lips as she studied his squirming.

"I'm nowhere near as accomplished as your last student. I would be a disappointment to you!" Everyone in the kingdom knew that Remus Johnstone had been her most treasured student. Rory's uncle had gray eyes that held many secrets, but he never spoke of his time in

Malaura's study, back when she'd ruled Avondale, and he'd been the gifted boy everyone was jealous of for catching the eye of the queen.

Now that her gaze rested on Adam, he squirmed as if that might scrape her attention off of him and cast it elsewhere.

She stroked Adam's arm, and he let out a whimper, his lips parted and trembling with terror. It was widely known that Malaura's Pulse was that she could touch a person and mirror their own Pulse. He felt her shooting his own ability of Persuasion and stripping away of inhibitions into him. "Tell me you'll come away with me and be my toy. I would take such care to train you properly. It's been so long since I've had a pupil worthy of my talents."

"No!" he blurted without filter, since his caution was gone. She'd meant to use his gift to convince him to run away with her, but it backfired, making him speak more honestly than his fear would normally permit. "You're disgusting! Even if you hadn't cursed Rory, I would never run away with you. Look at me, and then look at yourself! Your touch makes my skin crawl. I am not so desperate that I would give myself over to someone so plain as you." Adam shook his head and tried to rid himself of the Pulse he feared might cost him his life. He began to sweat through his suit. "Don't listen to a word I say! Take any room in the castle you like. Stay as long as you need. Only don't curse me!"

Malaura's red painted lips were drawn in a tight line. "Why would you assume you're in need of a curse?"

"I know your mind. Everyone knows Rory won't see her twenty-fifth birthday because of you."

Of all things, the woman laughed. "You do as you please without thinking of the consequences. Me, on the other hand, I only think of the consequences. What is the consequence of letting such selfishness carry on like this? What is the consequence of allowing such spoiled behavior to be idolized by the public?" Then she leaned in. "What is the consequence of letting you go for some other woman to enjoy your loveliness? Eyes that striking and a face that handsome should only be focused on me. If not me, then no one shall have you."

Adam swallowed and closed his eyes, lacing his fingers behind his head. "Please don't kill me."

"Silly boy. If I killed you, then how would you suffer for rejecting me and making me look like a fool by showing off my letters? I want you to live a long time regretting all we could have had together."

"No. No, please!"

She knelt before him and opened her fist, producing a handful of gold dust. Then she gripped the back of his head and forced his mouth upon hers, chortling through his blatant disgust, as if she enjoyed his distress. The moment she released him, she blew the gold dust into his face, smiling as he choked and coughed.

Adam sat back on his heels, still wiping the gold dust from his face. "What did you do to me?"

"Your insides will match your outsides now – horrifying as I've witnessed them to be."

An alarm rang through the house, and Adam guessed that Lucien had set off the fire alarm to get everyone out quicker. He rubbed the gold dust from his face, but recoiled, shouting with distress at the sight of his hands. "What are you doing to me? Make it stop!"

Brown hair sprouted from the backs of his hands, growing thick enough to make his pampered fingers appear animalistic. He felt around on his face, and found that his upper lip was now puffy, and his eyebrows were bushy and unruly.

The sorceress pressed her finger to his lips. "You'll remain ghastly like this until the last petal falls from this rose," she explained as she opened her fist again. This time, a perfect red bud bloomed out from the center of her palm. "You'll live ten more years like this while the slowly rose blooms. Then you'll join the Lupine tribe on your thirtieth birthday when the last petal falls. If I can't have you, I'll make it so that no one wants you."

Panicked, Adam shook his head, murmuring for her to reconsider.

Malaura remained firm in her judgment. "Our world has no place for selfishness like yours. You'll pay for your sins, and then you'll join the outcasts, roaming Avondale as a wolf until you die."

Audra burst into the foyer, eyes wild and arms raised to attack. Despite the danger, she was ready to risk it all to save Adam. "No! You'll not hurt my boy like this. His foolishness began when his parents died. This isn't who he'll always be."

The sorceress arose with a smile. "I'll hurt you all like this, unless you step aside."

Audra dropped to her knees and held Adam, who wailed into her shoulder, clawing at his hands in confusion. Instead of arguing with the woman, Audra closed her eyes and began a chant of her own, her arms shaking with determination that outweighed her fear. Though she'd been cast in the role of servant, she'd sat in on every one of Adam's lessons when he was schooled in the art of magic.

Then Lucien and Bosworth came forward, murmuring the same counter-curse in hopes of saving the boy they'd been entrusted to watch over. The other servants ran to Adam's aid, adding girth to the spell that needed to somehow be more powerful than the curse of the elite sorceress.

Malaura's head tilted back as she let out a hearty cackle. "Oh, how funny you are to try and counter a curse of mine. Only Remus was powerful enough to come up against me all those years ago, and that's only because I trained him. Enjoy the feeling of failure. In fact, for your petulance, I'll grant you with a curse of your own. The Lupine has no use for you all, but you'll be trapped until Adam turns, and then you'll be nothing."

She waved her hand over the foyer, and her voice grew louder as the servants collapsed, one by one as more of them ran forward to try and save the master of the house.

Adam saw precious little through the gold dust and the tears that marred his vision, but when he finally was able to look around, the sorceress had vanished, and the servants who loved him were nowhere to be seen.

Read *Beauty's Cursed Beast* today!

ABOUT THE AUTHOR

USA Today bestselling author Mary E. Twomey lives in Michigan with her three adorable children. She enjoys reading, writing, vegetarian cooking, and telling her children fantastic stories about wombats.

While she loves writing fantasy, dystopian, and paranormal tales for her readers, Mary also writes romance under the name Tuesday Embers, and cozy mysteries under the name Molly Maple.

Visit her online at www.maryetwomey.com, and sign up for her newsletter, so you never miss a new release.